FAKING ROMANCE

ROMANCES IN THE BUILDING SERIES
BOOK 1

S.E. ROSE

COPYRIGHT

Plot Assistance by The Fairy Plotmother
Editing by Judy's Proofreading
Couple Illustration © Celia Moscote
Cover Design by S.E. Rose

DEDICATION

To Amanda, for inspiring my main character. You pursued your dream and watching you do it has been a great joy. You're an amazing member of the book community and a true inspiration. I'm so very proud of you!

And to anyone who ever stumbled upon a found family. Sometimes the ones we surround ourselves with don't share our blood or a name, but they are just as important to our lives and our happiness.

CHAPTER ONE

Roxy

My mind swims with ideas as I twirl around the center of the empty space. I envision shelves full of romance novels and tables with fun T-shirts and stickers. This could work.

I'm not sure if it's the sweet old man standing next to me, the vibe of this art deco building, the fact that there's a studio apartment in the back, or the ease of access to downtown from here, but before I can think rationally, I turn to Mr. O'Brien.

"I'll take it!" I exclaim as I clap my hands together, unable to stop the childish joy from flowing through my extremities.

He gives me a big grin and nods. "Wonderful, Ms. Benedict. I'll have the lease agreement drawn up this afternoon," he says as he gives a wistful look around the place. I swear his eyes glaze over for a moment, but he blinks and with a stretch of his back turns toward the door.

This is crazy. I'm acting like a completely irrational adult human. Not only did I just agree to sign a lease on a storefront that I've only seen once, but I'm moving in here too. To be fair, I am dying to get out of my parents' home where I've been living since I made the epic mistake of moving in with the king of losers, as my father refers to my ex. And that's a fair name for him considering he's a cheating asshole. Prince Charming does not exist and I need to accept that. It's just a little hard to do when I'm about to open a romance bookstore. I want a happily ever after so badly. But the recent events in my life seem to indicate that I won't be getting one of those.

"Well, I'll have our cleaning crew come through once more and I'll set up a time to meet with our lawyers tomorrow if that works for you?" he says as he opens the door. A bell on the door jingles. I look up at it and he turns and follows my gaze. I see that sadness return for a fraction of a second. "I'll make sure they take that down," he adds.

I shake my head with a warm smile. "No, please leave it. I...it makes the space feel...homey," I try to explain because I do not know why I want the bell there. Maybe I've watched *You've Got Mail* too many times.

He returns my smile. "Will do, Ms. Benedict," he says as he holds out his hand to me.

I shake it. "Please, Mr. O'Brien, call me Roxy," I urge.

"Only if you call me Al," he states as he steps back.

"Well, Al, I'll see you tomorrow. I guess email me when you'd like to meet and where?" I say, though it comes out as a question.

"We can meet here. Say one p.m.? If that works for every-one," he offers as I walk over to my car. I managed to snag a street parking spot right in front of the building, although there was plenty of parking on this street since it dead-ends into a park.

"Great. I'll confirm with my lawyer, but that should work.

See you then," I reply. He nods and walks into a door next to the storefront, but pauses and turns back to me.

Al pulls out an old worn black leather wallet and removes a business card, handing it to me.

"This has my cell number and a QR code that has all my contact information," he says, adding emphasis on the QR code part as if I should be super impressed by this.

I press my lips together to keep from giggling. Al has to be at least eighty years old. He pats an old flip phone that's sticking out of his front pocket.

"Good to know," I say.

"And we can go over everything tomorrow, but I'm up on the sixth floor. And Jessa and Troy are on the fifth floor if there are any plumbing or electrical issues that need addressing," he reiterates for about the sixth time today.

"Got it," I answer.

"Well, see you tomorrow," he adds as he turns back to the door to the apartment building and goes inside.

I look up at the building. One eleven Hearts Lane.

It's a cute building, brick with a cream-and-green awning over the store's door and windows. It has six floors including the storefront level. Around the back, there's even a small courtyard and drive into a below-ground parking area for the residents. Getting a reserved parking spot in the city is an added bonus.

As my gaze looks from the top-floor windows down to the street level, a movement of a curtain on the second floor draws my attention. A chiseled jawline, straight nose, aquamarine eyes, and dark wavy hair peer out at me before the white curtains are drawn closed. Interesting...guess I'll have to meet my new neighbors this weekend. If I hadn't just taken a vow to stay away from all men for a while so I can get my shit together, I'd be more intrigued by the man who just looked down at me.

I turn to my right and look down at the end of the street. Something draws me toward a park bench a little ways down a trail that starts beneath a wrought iron trellis arch covered in wisteria. I leave my car and walk toward it. The bench faces away from the trail, by a small stream, the bank of it covered in wildflowers. It's surprisingly quiet here except for that bubbling stream sound that reminds me of the app I use to fall asleep.

I sit down on the bench next to a beautiful bouquet of roses. Glancing at the card attached to them, I use a single finger to open it.

"If you found these flowers, then the universe wants you to feel loved. Take them home and enjoy them. XOXO, The Guardian of Hearts Lane Park."

I look around but I'm the only one here. I bite my lip, unsure of whether to accept such an unanticipated gift. I've watched enough true crime shows to question if the flowers are laced with some sort of drug. I look at them again, but I see nothing suspicious. It would be nice to bring home flowers to my mom. She's put up with me for far too long.

Against my better judgment, I pick them up and walk back to my car. I survey the cute little side street once more. Yes, this is it. Out of the dozen commercial spaces I've looked at over the past six months, none of them remotely came close to this one. It's perfect in a quirky-old-building way.

———

Five months later...

Me: Jasp, I'm ready to move in.

My brother is helping me move into the studio apartment in the back of the shop today. Or at least he promised he would. Jasper is a busy guy. I've held off moving in as long as possible. The front shop hasn't needed a lot of work. I'm keeping the beautiful tin ceiling. I've begun painting the walls and slowly started building some furniture. I've ordered inventory and it's started to arrive. I haven't lived there yet, but after today, it'll be home and work.

I'd packed up my parents' old van that they used to use for road trips when we were younger. I'm shocked Dad kept it. And I'm more shocked that all my belongings fit inside it.

Jasper: I'll be over in an hour.

I put my phone back in my pocket and walk out to my car. I'd loaded up some things in here, so I could start organizing the studio apartment. Tomorrow, my sister Isla is coming over.

I glance at the park bench and see flowers sitting there. I'll have to check that out later.

Opening my car door, I glance up at the building and again find those aquamarine eyes peering down at me. I'm not sure what to make of this man. He doesn't seem very friendly by the scowl on his face. Is he mad that someone is moving in? Or maybe he's just an asshole?

Sighing, I reach into my car and pull out a box.

"Do you need help?" a woman's voice comes from beside me. I glance over and find a woman who I'd guess is around thirty years old. She is holding hands with a small girl, whose brown hair is in pigtails with big red bows on them. I've just been in and out on quick trips over the past few months as I've checked in on things, so I haven't met any of my new neighbors aside from Mr. O'Brien and Troy, who handles the maintenance for the building.

"Oh, uh, I got it," I assure her.

She smiles at me. "I'm Carly and this is my daughter, Ava. We live in number four," she says as she points to the building.

"I'm"—I shift the box back in the car and extend my hand —"Roxy," I say.

"Nice to meet you, Roxy. I heard you were moving into the first-floor apartment and you're renting the store space," she adds as we shake hands.

"Yep. Hi, Ava," I say to the little girl.

She looks up at me quizzically. "Do you have any dead bodies in there?" she asks as she glances at the box.

I frown. "Nope," I reply slowly, my brows furrowing in confusion.

"Sorry...she's apparently been listening to the true crime podcast I've had on in the car," Carly says with a grimace.

I laugh. "No worries."

"Al says you're opening a bookstore," Carly adds.

"Yes. A romance bookstore," I specify.

She grins. "I'll look forward to shopping there, then." She pauses as Ava continues to crane her neck to look inside my car, clearly uncertain whether I'm lying about the dead bodies.

"I guess, we'll be seeing you, then," she says.

"Yep. Nice meeting you again," I say as I lift the box and head inside, walking back to my apartment.

My phone rings as I look around the kitchenette and living space of the small studio.

Glancing down, I see Isla's name.

"Hey, how is the place?" she asks.

"Well, it's great," I state as I take in the small space that has a door leading out to the courtyard.

"Meet any hot neighbors?" she asks and I already know she's waggling her eyebrows.

"Really?"

"For me, not you," she assures me.

"Just the mysterious grumpy man in the window, but we haven't met yet," I explain. "I've seen him peeking out of his curtains at least three other times. But my visits tend to be short and I haven't had any other interactions with him."

"A mystery, love it," she says.

"Yeah, just met a nice woman and her daughter who asked if I had any dead bodies in the car," I add.

Isla coughs as she starts laughing. "Shit, warn me before you say stuff like that. I just inhaled my soda."

"There's also the mystery of those flowers..." I trail off as I walk out the store's door and down the street toward the park.

"What flowers?" she asks.

"The ones on the park bench," I remind her. I've seen them there a few other times since that first day. They always have the same note attached.

"You brought those home for Mom," she says in confusion.

"I did, but there are more here again," I reply as I walk over and read the card on the flowers. Same as before.

"Interesting," she says.

I head back to my car. "That's one way of putting it," I say as I open my car door to grab a bag.

"This place sounds...interesting," she says again.

"You already said that," I groan.

"Yep. OK, I gotta run. See you tomorrow," she says as she disconnects.

I look back up at the building. One-eleven Hearts Lane, you really do have some mysteries. I just hope building a business here isn't going to be one of them.

CHAPTER TWO

Grayson

I swipe my bow over the strings of the cello and feel my body relax as the notes fill the air. I've been working on this piece for hours, wanting each instrument to sound perfect. I'm nearly there when a loud banging comes from beneath me, jarring me from my musical world into the stark reality of the real one I live in.

I was weary of the woman who rented the commercial space below me. I had to yell at Troy a few times when he was making noise down there, but he tries to get things done when I'm not working since he knows my schedule. Al has tried at least a half dozen times to reassure me that she's the perfect tenant to take on the space formerly occupied by his late wife's antique shop.

I long for the antique shop. I've only been here a little over two years, but that first year was perfect. Edith was quiet and kind. Aside from that damn bell on the door ringing on the rare occasion that someone came in, she made nearly zero noise. And then she died.

That was brutal...for everyone in the building. Edith was like family and losing her left a gaping hole in all our hearts. Her old age and life well-lived were the only things that kept us sane during those first few months.

I didn't think I could become so connected to a building and the people residing in it. In the world I come from, relationships are transactions. And transactions come at a high cost.

With a shake of my head to clear my thoughts, I start again but an immediate bang has me setting down my beloved instrument and heading straight out the door and downstairs.

I walk outside and press the door of the shop to enter it, but it doesn't budge. I lean forward and peer inside and see two women nailing something to a wall.

I pound on the glass, but no response.

What in the actual fuck?

I pound again and one of them looks over at me. She looks a little younger than me with long blonde wavy hair that's pulled up in a ponytail on top of her head. Her giant blue eyes stare back at mine and widen a little before she steps off a ladder and walks toward me, pulling out an earbud as she does.

She unlocks the door and pushes it open.

"Hi," she says meekly, looking up from beneath dark lashes. She might be gorgeous, but I don't give a fuck right now.

"Hello. I'm Grayson Porter," I state as I stretch out my hand deciding to try to be civil first. "I live upstairs, right above your shop."

"Oh, right." She wipes her hand on her pants and shakes mine. Her skin is warm and smooth and a zing of static passes between us. She retracts her hand, clearly feeling it too. "I'm Roxy Benedict. I just moved in. It's nice to meet you."

The other woman begins hammering what looks like a bookcase.

"Isla, can you stop for like two seconds?" Roxy asks before looking back at me. "Sorry, that's my sister Isla. She's helping me get the shop sorted."

"Well, about that. I'm trying to finish writing a piece..." I trail off taking a deep breath. "I'm a composer and a musician and I sort of need it to be quiet."

"Oh. Uh, yeah. Sorry about that. I swear the hammering is almost done. Maybe we can take a break for a few hours," she offers.

I nod. "Thank you. If you could, that would be very help-ful." I look around. "What exactly is your store going to be?

She smiles proudly and holds up her arms. "A romance bookstore."

I frown as I try to comprehend the meaning. "I'm sorry...a what?"

"A bookstore for romance readers," she reiterates as one eyebrow shoots up as if she's assessing my reaction to this information.

"Right..." I say slowly with a small shake of my head. "Do people actually buy that many of those books to make that a profitable store?"

She sighs. "Yes. Yes, they do."

"Right. Anyhow, I need total silence for at least two more hours," I state as I look over her head at the store, still unsure how anyone could make a living off romance books.

"Sure. We can finish the painting instead," she offers.

Fuck. Painting might be worse than the noise.

"Could you maybe do something else? And paint tomor-row?" I ask.

Now she's the one frowning. "Why?"

"Paint fumes give me migraines," I state, with a sigh of exhaustion. Actually, I feel one coming on right now.

"Fine, we'll set up furniture," she grumbles like a petulant child.

"Will there be hammering involved with that?" I ask from behind gritted teeth because the fact that I have to ask her to be neighborly is putting me in a mood.

"No," she growls and pauses as she opens the door to walk back inside. "It was nice meeting you, Mr. Porter." But the way she says it tells me she thinks it was anything but nice, and honestly, I feel the same. I don't want to look for another apartment. I was here first.

And with that she closes it, leaving me on the other side, inhaling her perfume that slowly dissipates after a few seconds. I run a hand through my hair as I turn and press the key code to get back into the building.

Trudging up to my apartment, I pass Carly on the steps.

"Hey," I mutter.

"What's wrong?" she asks, pausing mid-step and looking down at me from the landing on the second floor.

I walk up to her and lean on the wall. "That new woman downstairs is making a shit ton of noise."

"When do you have to get your composition to the producer?" she asks. The entire building is aware that I'm in the running to compose music for a film. It's something I've wanted to do for over a year, and after networking way more than I ever wanted to, it was my family name that got me a meeting with a well-known Hollywood producer. He agreed to listen to a sample I'm making based on a film concept he shared. The film is just about to wrap up in the coming weeks. This could be my big break. I walked away from my family and their fortune to pursue this dream and being so close to getting what I want has me laser-focused. I'm so close to making my dream come true, I can practically taste it.

"Tomorrow," I answer.

Carly hugs me and I hug her back.

"You got this, Gray. Go finish it. You're going to kick some ass. I just know he'll love it. You are meant to do this," she says as she pulls back, giving me a giant smile.

"Thanks, Carly. I'm just stressed and I'm used to the quiet here and...well..." I trail off.

"I know. But remember, she's new and she doesn't know any of us yet. Cut her some slack, OK?" Carly suggests.

Shrugging, I start up the stairs. "Where's Ava?" I ask, realizing that Carly's nearly five-year-old sidekick is missing.

"She has a playdate with a little girl we met at the park a few weeks ago. It turns out I went to high school with the kid's mom. How wild is that? Anyhow, it is giving me four whole hours to run errands with no child. I'm not sure I'm going to know what to do with myself," she says with a laugh as she continues walking downstairs.

"I don't want to see you on an episode of *Moms Gone Wild*," I tease as I open my door at the landing.

"Funny, Gray. Real funny," she retorts and I hear the outside door swing open. Somehow, my little interaction with Carly has me feeling lighter than a few minutes ago.

Fuck my family. This one I found is so much better.

———

I hit send on the file. I've worked through most of the night in the makeshift recording studio I made out of my walk-in closet. It's not perfect, but it'll have to do for now. I couldn't get time at my friend's recording studio, and frankly, I don't need the demo to be that polished yet. But I do want it to be good and I think what I just sent was damn near perfect.

I breathe a sigh of relief and decide to go for a walk. I take my travel mug of coffee and start down the Hearts Lane Park trail. The flowers are sitting on the bench as always.

I snap a photo and send it to the building group chat.

Me: (photo) Are we ever going to solve this mystery?

Brayden: I sort of dig keeping it a mystery.

Carly: I'm on Team Leave It a Mystery.

Hutch: No way, inquiring minds need to know.

Drew: I propose a stakeout.

Cam: You and Hutch propose a stakeout every time we discuss this. Just do it already.

I laugh. Drew Whiteford and Camryn Tanner are roommates, so I know they'll be discussing this later. Carly Maxwell and Brayden Murphy live in the two apartments on floor three. They have been friends ever since Carly moved in with Ava, who was just a toddler at the time. And Hutchinson or Hutch Cromwell is my neighbor on the second floor. They are all wonderful people. And along with our other neighbors, we've been speculating on the mysterious flowers for years. People have stayed out looking at the bench but no one has ever seen the flowers delivered here. So the neighborhood lore continues.

I have half a mind to take the flowers today. Why not? Men never get flowers and it's a big day for me. So I pick them up on my way back.

I'm just about to the building door when my mug splashes coffee on my pants.

"Shit," I mutter as I try to brush it away. I'm not paying attention and run smack into someone. I look up to meet the gaze of Ms. Benedict. Great. Just what I needed.

"Oh, sorry," she says as I stand back to my full height and look down at her.

She's holding paint cans.

"Are you doing that today?" I grimace.

She nods. "Yeah, remember you asked that I do it today instead of yesterday. It's just the trim. Everything else is already painted."

I fucking did ask that, but shit, I'd just like to chill at the apartment today. If I lived a few stories up, then I'd probably avoid the smell altogether, but not right above it.

"So I did," I mutter.

"Cool, well, I'll be starting shortly," she adds as she sets down a can and opens the shop door. I glance inside as the window and door are now covered in brown paper. There are rows of shelves lining two of the three walls and some smaller shelves by what I think is going to be a checkout table. I see boxes with stickers on them that appear to be more tables that need to be put together.

If I was a nicer man, I'd offer to help her, but not with paint fumes. And honestly, she's annoying the hell out of me, so it's better if I can keep my distance.

I start to say thanks for stopping the noise yesterday, but she shuts the door in my face. Well, I guess it's going to be like that. Shaking my head, I decide to pay Margie and Cornelia a visit. The fourth floor should be far enough away from the fumes. And my two favorite elderly ladies have been asking me to help them get a subscription service on their television for a month now.

I walk up to their apartment, deciding not to take the rickety old elevator that seems to break at least once a month. It's one of the reasons I love the second floor.

I don't even knock before Margie opens the door.

"Well, look what the cat dragged in. You turn in that new tune you wrote?" she asks as she opens her door and ushers me inside.

"Yep. It's done," I confirm as I plop down on her sofa next to Cornelia who is knitting what looks like the world's longest scarf.

"You meet our new neighbor yet?" Cornelia asks, not bothering to look up at me.

"I did."

She glances over at me from above her giant tortoiseshell-framed lenses that magnify her eyes. "And?"

"She's opening a romance bookstore," I state, deciding to withhold sharing my initial judgment. I'm not one for gossip, well, not normally.

"I saw her yesterday. Pretty little thing," Margie says from the perch on her favorite leather chair that has seen better days.

"You don't like her?" Cornelia asks.

"No, I didn't say that." Fuck, did I say that? No. I wouldn't.

"Uh-huh," Cornelia mumbles and looks back down at her world record–length scarf.

"I didn't. She just...makes a lot of noise," I try to explain for reasons I don't understand except these two little old women are good at putting me in my place and I both hate that and love that about them.

"Gray, dear, she is moving in and opening a business. That's not exactly an activity that is noise-free," Margie points out as she leans back and takes a long sip of one of her herbal teas that she drinks all day.

"Margie has a point," Cornelia agrees.

"Well, I didn't say I had an opinion yet. It's just been noisy," I try to argue.

"Just mind your manners. We know you can get grumpy but she doesn't know you yet. And you should always lead with a good impression. You just never know if someone could be 'the one,'" Margie states with a nod.

"Yes, ma'am. But I highly doubt that she's going to be anything but a neighbor." I look toward the new television that Cornelia won at the community bingo night a month ago. "OK, let's get you all sorted so you can watch Netflix," I add, trying to change the conversation to a different topic.

"Netflix and chill. Isn't that what the kids call it?" Cornelia says as she motions to the television with a knitting needle.

"I heard it's code for something else," Margie says with a wicked smirk.

I groan. "Ladies, it just means to watch Netflix and literally chill." I start going through controls and setting up their account. But my mind keeps wandering back to Roxy. Did I overreact? Maybe. Was she accommodating? I guess so. Whatever, as long as she's quiet from here out, I guess I'll survive.

I snort to myself. Romance bookstore. Who believes in romance anymore? Seriously, everyone just right-swipes on their phone. She'll probably be out of here within six months tops.

At that thought I smile to myself and start showing my adoptive grannies what Netflix shows to watch.

CHAPTER THREE

Roxy

"You're hired," I say to the fifth person I've interviewed today. She's the first one I've felt a vibe with and she's also smart, funny, and has a great résumé.

"Seriously?" Jocelyn Martinez asks, her eyes going wide.

"Yeah. I mean, I can only put you on part-time for the first three months, but I'm hoping by month four I can increase your hours," I explain for the second time since the interview began.

She studies me with her big brown eyes for a long beat and then holds out a hand. "I accept," she says, her rosy lips tipping up into a big, toothy smile.

I shake her hand. "Welcome aboard," I reply.

Jocelyn is a graduate student at a nearby university. She's studying literature and wants to be a teacher or a professor. Her favorite genre is romance. We spent most of the interview discussing our favorite books. And by her third favorite,

I knew she would make the perfect employee for my bookstore.

She looks around us. I started ordering books and merchandise last week and the boxes have begun arriving. I haven't even started organizing anything yet.

"You really don't want me to start until you open in a few weeks, because it looks like you could use the help," she says as she stands and walks over to a table of boxes.

I look around us. I have all the furniture set up. The paint is dry on the walls. All my financial stuff is set up and I'm moved into the small studio apartment in the back. It's essentially ready to go other than getting everything out and doing inventory.

"Maybe you can come in on Friday?" I suggest as I realize that I probably do need her to work a day or two before we open. "I won't be able to pay you at the rate we discussed until we're open," I explain. I have already opened our online store, but that is just part of the income for my small business and not nearly enough to pay my bills, the store's bills, and an employee.

She waves me off as she looks inside a box sitting near her. She squeals. "I've been dying to read this book. I didn't think it came out for another week."

"Yeah. I know someone at the publisher and they got me a box of them. I can't sell them until after next week, which works out since we won't open until after the release date."

"That's awesome. I definitely want to buy one...with my employee discount," she adds with a smirk.

I shake my head and laugh. "I'll set one aside for each of us."

"Sweet. OK, well, I'm going to head out to class. I'll see you Friday. I guess let me know what time," she says as she makes her way to the door.

"Will do. I'll get all the paperwork together and we can fill that out, then," I say. She nods as she leaves and I sit back down. Holy shitballs! I just hired my first employee. I can't believe I'm actually doing this.

I pull out my phone and text my one and only true friend, Taylor Perkins.

Me: I just hired an employee!

Tay: Holy crap! You're like a real businesswoman! I'm so proud of you!

Me: IRK (big eyes emoji)

Tay: I wish I could be there for your opening day. (Sad face emoji)

Me: Me too (crying emoji)

Tay: I promise I'll come see the store as soon as I'm stateside.

Me: You better!

Tay: Pinky promise.

I smile and set my phone down. Taylor just took a job in Spain as an English teacher. I'm thrilled for her, but I'm also sad that I won't see her for at least six months. I really need to make some more friends.

I text my sibling chat next. I'm the second oldest of four kids. My older sister, Cybil, lives in New York City and teaches economics at NYU. My brother, Jasper, works for a big software company and does analytics or something. I never really understand his job when he tries to explain it. And my little sister, Isla, goes to the same grad school as Jocelyn where she's studying marketing. They are all super successful and smart. Meanwhile, I barely graduated college with a degree in communications. I have had a string of jobs, almost as long as my list of guys I've gone on one date with aside from Richard, my jerk ex. I can't seem to get either of those things right. So when our grandmother died and left us each some money, I decided to do something totally crazy. My family thinks I'm making a big mistake by sinking my inheritance into a bookstore, but I felt stifled living with my parents and I knew if I didn't try making my passion a reality, I'd always regret it. So here I am, trying to make one of my dreams come true. I just hope I don't fail.

––––––

A knock on my door has me pulling my head out of a box of books. I walk over and open the door to find Carly standing there.

"Hey, I'm not sure if Al told you, but we have a weekly happy hour up on the roof if you want to stop by. It starts at five," she says.

"Oh, I..." I trail off as I look down at my watch and then over at my boxes. It's quarter till five. I should keep going but a drink and social interaction sounds like a better plan. Al had mentioned something about Thursday happy hours, but I'd forgotten. I've been so busy that I haven't met most of the people in the building yet. I don't want anyone else mad at me over noises, so it'd probably be best to get to know them in a friendly setting just in case other people end up with concerns like Mr. Porter. "Uh, sure, yeah, I'll come up."

"Cool. I just need to go get Ava and then I'll meet you up there," she says with a wave.

I wave back and then finish going through a box of romantasy books before I head up to the roof. I'm embarrassed to admit that I don't know how to get up there. I start up the stairs and nearly run into someone as I turn the corner to walk up the next flight.

I start to flail backward and strong hands grab my shoulders.

"Whoa!" a voice says as my eyes trail up to meet...Grayson Porter. Fuck.

"Uh, sorry, I...uh..." I trail off unsure of what to say.

"Where's the fire?" he asks, looking around.

I frown. "I'm running up the stairs, not down."

"Right." He smirks.

I fight every instinct to roll my eyes. Why does this man have the uncanny ability to get under my skin? First, he starts his introduction to me with a complaint and now he has the audacity to tease me. What the hell?

I step back and his hands release me. "Well, uh, I guess I'll see you later," I say as I continue walking up the next flight of stairs as fast as I can to get away from Mr. Grumpypants Porter.

I get to the top landing and look around. I see a door that I think goes to Al's apartment and then another door. I push it open and find a narrow set of stairs with a door up at the top of them. I walk up them, hoping I found the right way to the roof. How have I not explored the building yet? I've been here for almost two weeks.

I slowly turn the doorknob and push. A sigh of relief leaves me as I hear people chatting. The warm summer air circles around me, enveloping me like a hug. I step onto what appears to be a patio made of wood as I look around me. There's a raised platform with a hot tub. It's gated off and the hot tub has a cover on it. There's a greenhouse that looks brimming with plants. There's a covered deck area that has...an outdoor kitchen and bar. Damn, this place is great.

Al is behind the bar, with a martini shaker in one hand and a frosted glass in the other. A man sits on a barstool in front of him, and he is enormous like he could take on two or three men in a fight and win, hands down. He has blondish hair, but aside from that, all I can see is his huge-ass body.

There's a tall man sitting next to him with dark hair. At a table near the bar, two little old ladies sit chatting with Jessa and Troy Fletcher who I already know. I'm happy to see Troy.

He's helped a lot with little things in the store that needed fixing.

I start to walk over when the door flies open, nearly sending me across the roof. I turn to find Grayson staring at me. Of course, it's fucking Grayson Porter again. Can I not start running into another neighbor?

"Maybe try standing not in front of doors," he suggests as he walks past me to join the other two men at the bar.

I try not to narrow my eyes at him as I begin walking over to say hi to Al O'Brien.

The door opens again and a woman with curly red hair and a short, thin man with perfectly sculpted brown hair walk through the doorway.

"Oh, you must be Roxy," the woman says as her eyes lock with mine.

"Uh, guilty," I answer.

She holds out her hand. "I'm Cam and this is my roommate, Drew. We live on the fifth floor in number eight. It's nice to meet you."

I shake her hand and then Drew's.

"Nice to meet you both," I reply as Carly and Ava come out the door.

"Oh good, you met Cam and Drew. Ava, go have Mr. Al make you a Shirley Temple," she says as she pats her daughter's butt, shoving her in the direction of the bar. I watch Ava run over and the large man scoops her up in his arms. She sits on his lap and begins speaking with the other man.

"Come on. We'll introduce you to everyone," Carly says as she links arms with me. "Well, everyone but Kasen. He's away for work again. But you'll probably see his cousin, Elliott. He feeds Kasen's sea anemones every week."

I stop walking. "Sea anemones?"

She nods. "Don't ask. Kasen is...unique." I nod and we continue walking. She takes me over to the bar.

"Hutch, Bray, this is Roxy, our newest resident and owner of what is going to be a romance bookstore."

"Nice to meet you," the large man says. "I'm Hutch Cromwell."

Hutch Cromwell. Why does that sound familiar? I give him a big smile. "Nice to meet you, Hutch."

"And I'm Brayden Murphy," says the man next to him. I reach over Ava to shake his hand.

"Grayson," I acknowledge my neighbor and apparent mortal enemy.

Grayson nods toward me but busies himself with his phone. Whatever.

"What'll it be?" Al asks as he tosses a dish towel on his shoulder.

"I didn't know you were a bartender," I tease.

He laughs. "My wife, Edith, and I always loved any excuse to host friends."

Cam leans toward me. "Try his apple martini."

"OK, I'll have an apple martini," I state as I lean on the countertop of the bar.

"Coming right up," Al replies as he gets to work making my drink. He sets two martini glasses down and splits the drink between them.

"Thanks, Al," Cam says as she takes the one closest to her.

He nods and hands me mine. "Enjoy. I'm glad Carly grabbed you. I completely forgot to remind you about happy hour."

"No worries," I assure him as Cam motions for me to follow her. We walk over to the table with what I assume are more neighbors.

"Everyone, this is Roxy," she says as she motions to me like I'm a letter on the board of *Wheel of Fortune*.

"This is Margie and Cornelia. They live on the fourth

floor in number seven. And this is Jessa and Troy Fletcher. They help Al run the building," she says with a wave of her hand.

"Hi, Troy and Jessa." I turn to Carly. "We've met. Troy has helped get the store fixed up." Turning back to the older women, I add, "Nice to meet you all."

"Lovely to meet you, dear," Cornelia says.

"Everything OK in the apartment?" Troy asks.

"Oh, uh, yes. Everything is great." I smile before taking a sip of the martini. "Damn, that is good," I add.

"Told you," Cam says.

Drew pulls over a chair and pats it. "Have a seat and tell us all about you. We love gossip."

I nearly choke on my drink. "I—I'm sorry, what?"

Cam laughs. "What Drew means is that we don't get new tenants very often, so he's excited to meet you. Right, Drew?" She glares at him.

Drew shrugs and fingers the rim of his glass. "Something like that. A romance bookstore, huh?" His eyes meet mine.

"Do you like romance novels?" I ask him.

"Oh, honey, Drew reads books that make *Fifty Shades of Grey* look tame," Margie says with a giggle.

"Fuck off, Marge, you practically devoured the last series I gave you," he teases.

And just like that, I start to fall in love with my new neighbors.

CHAPTER FOUR

Grayson

"Make it a generous pour," I say to Al as he grabs the bottle of whiskey from beneath the bar top.

"Rough day?" he asks, raising one bushy white eyebrow.

"Did you hear anything yet about the film?" Brayden asks.

Hutch leans forward to look around Brayden. "I heard you working on it. The guy's an idiot if he turns it down."

Al pushes the glass toward me, and I take a long sip. "I haven't heard anything yet," I tell them before taking another drink. I wish they'd change the conversation. I'm nervous as fuck. I've worked so hard to get a chance and this could be my big break. I feel my knee start to bounce with nerves as I down the rest of the expensive whiskey.

"Slow down, kid. I'm sure you'll get it," Al murmurs as he pours me more of the amber liquid.

"Hopefully," I manage as I glance over at my new neighbor. She's only been here an hour and Roxy has already made best friends with half the building. She's sitting on the arm of an Adirondack chair that Drew is occupying. Her hands are animated as she explains the plot of some book to Drew, Jessa, Margie, Cam, and Cornelia.

"So what do you think of her?" Carly asks me. I feel Al looking at me. I turn to find both of them leaning on the bar, watching me expectantly from the far side of the wooden table. Hutch and Bray also look my way.

"She's loud," I state because it's true and it doesn't give much away. The truth of the matter is, I don't know what I think of her yet. I was annoyed with her noise, but I could also tell she wasn't intentionally trying to be a rude neighbor. She just seemed oblivious, which in my anxious state is not welcomed. I almost feel bad for snapping at her, almost.

Carly rolls her eyes. "No, seriously, what do you think?"

Al leans in toward Carly. "She's gorgeous. Don't you think?" he asks us both.

"Yep," Carly agrees. My eyes follow their gaze back to Roxy. Her long blonde hair sways as she finishes her story and starts laughing at something Drew says. She leans back and her blue dress rides up her thighs, revealing more creamy flesh. Her eyes sparkle and the blue color of her irises seems enhanced by the bright blue dress. Her red lips are turned up, exposing perfectly straight, white teeth. Freckles dot her nose and cheeks. Her nails are painted a color that matches her lips. I can't deny it. She's indeed beautiful.

I decide I don't need my friends to know my thoughts about that yet. So, I shrug.

"Yeah, she's pretty," I say as nonchalantly as I can muster.

Carly leans over and slaps the back of my head.

"Ouch! What was that for?" I groan as I rub my head. I glance back over to see Drew taking his empty glass and coming toward us.

Ava giggles from where she's still sitting on Hutch's lap,

playing a never-ending game of tic-tac-toe with Brayden, who pulls out a fifth napkin to start again.

"Ava, never hit people," Carly says looking around my head at her daughter.

"OK, Mommy," Ava whispers as she tries not to laugh.

"Unless they are being idiots," Brayden says as he also smacks my head.

"Shit, guys. Cut it out," I hiss.

They all laugh. "Oh, come on. I've only met her for a few minutes and even I admit she's gorgeous," Hutch says as he glances over at her.

Drew leans on the counter. "Who's gorgeous?" he asks, batting his eyes.

"Our new neighbor," Brayden states while keeping his eye on the board. "Ava! That's cheating."

"No, it's not," she protests, crossing her arms.

He groans as he scratches out the move she just made for him and blocks her.

"Who doesn't think she's gorgeous?" Drew asks, looking down the bar at all of us while holding his empty glass up for Al to refill.

"Gray," Hutch says under his breath.

Drew glares at me. "You are so full of shit."

I give him a pointed look because Drew is gay and he also is dating someone.

He glares back at me. "I'm gay. Not blind," he quips.

"Whatever. I said she was pretty," I say. I'm about to change the subject when my phone pings. Everyone stares down at it.

Slowly, I pick it up. It's a text from none other than Pierce Pointer, the producer I sent my demo to only a few days ago.

Pierce: Hey, man. I listened to the demo. You got a minute to chat?

"I need to make a call," I say to everyone and no one as I

stand and walk over to the side of the bar area where it's quiet.

I hit call on my phone and Pierce picks up right away.

"You ready for greatness?" he asks.

I frown because I don't get what he's saying.

"Because I am going to make you a household name, my friend. That demo was fucking amazing. Wade and I love it! And we're both in agreement. You're it. We both want that to be *the* song of the film. Hell, I don't even think we need lyrics. Just that melody. You have no idea how relieved I am to have found the right music. Wade and I were beginning to worry we'd never find it," he states.

My jaw falls open. I did it. I can't fucking believe I did it. I was worried that Wade Humphreys, the music supervisor for the film, wouldn't be as sold on my music as Pierce, but I guess I was wrong.

"Wow. I, uh, thanks," I stammer as I try to compose myself.

"Sure thing. I'm having a little post-filming party at Dot's Bar on Twelfth Street next Tuesday around six. I'd love for you to come by," he says.

"Oh, I..." I trail off as I try to think about what my schedule is next week. I have four contracted performances with the city orchestra, but I can't remember which dates.

"Not just you. If you have a girlfriend, feel free to bring her," he says, as though he thought that was my reason for hesitating.

Fuck. "Oh, uh, sure. Yeah. I'll do that," I say. Before I even think, the words are out of my mouth. Double fuck.

"Wonderful, can't wait to meet her. I'll have Haven with me," he says, referencing his wife.

"Great," I say as I still try to wrap my head around the fact that I just told this guy I have a girlfriend, or I implied it.

"OK, see you then. We can talk more logistics over a

beer," he says and then hangs up, leaving me staring at my phone.

"So?" Al asks as he walks over to me.

"I got it," I say, my focus still on the electronic device in my hand.

I don't even notice the silence until my friends erupt with cheers. Hutch tosses Ava in the air and she squeals and giggles. "Mr. Gray is gonna be famous!" he says to her and laughs some more.

Suddenly, I'm surrounded by my friends as they hug me and clap me on the back. After a few minutes and a hundred questions, we're interrupted by the pizza delivery guy, Tony Jr., who has our usual order of two cheese, two pepperoni, and one veggie pizza with two sides of garlic and cheese bread.

Everyone lunges for the food, but Al hangs back with me, putting a reassuring hand on my shoulder.

"What's wrong, Gray?" he asks.

I look down at him. "I may have implied that I have a girl-friend, and he invited me and this *girlfriend* to a party next Tuesday."

"Just pretend you broke up," he suggests with a shrug of his shoulders.

I shake my head. "That'd be weird. It'd be more obvious that I lied."

"So, just call a woman on one of those dating apps that you kids are always talking about," Al offers.

I don't have the heart to tell Al that I haven't been on any dating app ever. I had girlfriends in college and high school. I was only single for a year or so before Lydia and I started dating and now it's been almost a year since we broke up. I've gone out with a few women that Hutch, Kasen, or Brayden set me up with, but none of them worked out.

"I don't want to do that," I reply.

Al cocks his head to one side. "I think I have a young woman who would be a great fake girlfriend for you. I'll give her a call and have her meet you at this party. Just give me the details."

I eye him suspiciously. First, how does Al know any single, young women? Two, why not just give me her number? Three, I'm supposed to pretend to be dating someone for a while on a blind date with them? Is he for real?

"Trust me, OK?" he urges with a wink and a pat on my back.

I can't believe I'm agreeing to this. I have got to be crazy. Or desperate. Or both.

"Yeah, alright. But, Al"—I pause as I look at him—"she has to understand it's just a short-term fake thing."

"Of course, of course," he assures me with a smile and walks back over to join our friends as they dig into the pizzas.

I stand there for a few seconds as I consider the events of the last twenty minutes. Everything is going to be different now. I've done it. I actually made this music career work. I text the only family member that I still regularly speak with, my sister.

Me: My music got approved by the producer.

Adriana: OMG! Congrats! That's awesome. Maybe that'll help Mom and Dad come around.

Me: Highly doubt that.

Adriana: You never know.

Me: I won't be holding my breath over here.

Adriana: Still, I'm proud of you.

Me: Thanks, Ad.

I put my phone in my pocket. My parents disowned me when I told them I wasn't going to be part of their family business and would instead be pursuing music. I won't lie. A part of me would love to rub it in their faces. But first, I need signed contracts...and a fake girlfriend.

CHAPTER FIVE

Roxy

I sit on the floor surrounded by a pile of boxes with Jocelyn next to me. She's sorting merch and I'm sorting books. I've had so much delivered here over the past few months, but the real work has been these last few weeks.

Troy is here installing a new light fixture. Al had saved some antique chandeliers from his wife's store and offered them up for the store. They are gorgeous and perfectly in line with the vibe I'm going for.

"Hey, you want a coffee?" I ask as I glance at my watch. We've been at it for three hours.

"Sure," she says, not looking up from where she is entering quantities of stickers she's unboxing into my inventory database.

"I'll be back." I get up and dust off my jeans. I make my way across the street to a little café where I discovered Cam works.

She looks up as I walk inside.

"Hey," she greets me with a smile.

"Hi. Can I get two..." I trail off as I read the sign written in chalk behind her. "Caramel mocha lattes?" I finish.

"Coming right up. You should try our double-fudge muffins. I added a little something extra in them and they are amazeballs," she says as she gets to work making our drinks.

"Sure. I'll take two," I say as I look around the café. It's a bakery that serves coffee. There are dozens of types of pastries and cakes under the glass of the display case. I've stopped over here a few times this week.

"So, how are things?" I ask, trying to make small talk while she finishes frothing some milk.

"Good. The owner of this place is looking to sell it," she leans over the counter. "I think I might try to buy it."

"Seriously?" I ask.

She shrugs and goes back to making the lattes. "Yeah. I have just enough saved that I might be able to put down some and pay the rest with a small business loan."

"Well, having just done some of that myself, I have plenty of tips. So let me know if you need any help," I offer.

The door to the café opens and Carly walks inside.

"I need a double macchiato and two triple-chocolate oatmeal cookies, STAT," she declares as she walks over and leans on the bar top at the end of the counter.

"Rough day?" Cam inquires with a raised eyebrow.

"You have no idea. Ava lost her first tooth because some kid at daycare pushed her down and she knocked it out on a dollhouse. She freaked out. I had to leave work and take her to the dentist. Brayden offered to watch her so I could come get coffee. He said I needed a chill moment. And he's not wrong," she says as she pushes some hair out of her face.

Cam points to our right. "I think you're in the wrong place. Go to Joe's."

I giggle. Even being new, I know that Joe's is a local tavern two doors down from the café.

Carly rolls her eyes. "Can't. Brayden has a shift later, so I need to mom again in about an hour. I'm just hoping Ava will go to sleep tonight and then I can sit in silence and drink a glass of wine and watch the latest season of *Love Is Blind*."

"OMG! It's so good. Have you started it yet?" I ask.

She shakes her head.

I pretend to zipper my lips closed. "I won't say a word, but we must debrief when you finish."

Laughing, she pulls her phone out and checks it. "Noted." She looks up at me. "How's everything going with the bookstore? I saw a sign in the window that it's opening soon."

I nod. "I can't believe it." I sigh. "I wish I had more time to get acclimated here, but I really need the income. I can't wait any longer. It's just a bummer that I haven't had time to do anything else. I've barely unpacked. I haven't even tried going on a dating app in like a month." I sigh.

"You need a date?" Carly asks, putting her phone down.

I shrug. "I mean, part of me has sworn off men, because... ewww. But another part of me can't wait to find my happily ever after. I suppose if I don't put myself out there, I won't ever be able to find my perfect book boyfriend?"

Carly laughs and looks at Cam and back at me. "What's your type?"

"Oh, uh, I don't know if I have one," I admit as I try to think of what I want in a guy. "I mean. He needs to be funny, kind, financially stable, not a psycho, and smart."

Carly taps her cheek. "OK, well, in our building there's Kasen. He's sort of got this mysterious air about him. He works in cybersecurity. He travels a lot for work. Come to think of it, I haven't seen him in a few weeks. So he must be working. He's ex-military and he's sort of quiet. But he's definitely attractive."

"He's superhot," Cam states with a laugh as she pretends to fan herself.

I giggle. "OK, so the hot-and-silent type?"

"Yes. And there's Hutch. Hutch is such a sweetie. He's a total...what do they call it?" Carly continues.

"He's a cinnamon roll guy," Cam interjects as she sets my drinks down. I grin. I love that she's using book terminology.

"He's a former football player. He was injured. He's really sweet. And then there's Brayden. He's a really good guy, like the absolute best. I don't know what I'd do without him. He's always got my back when I need help with Ava or anything at all. And lastly, there's Gray. He can come off a little harsh, but he's a solidly good person. He's loyal as heck and he's really talented," Carly finishes.

"I don't know if I want to date someone in our building, per se. But good to know," I say as I pay Cam and take my order, walking toward the door.

"Never say never. But I get it," Carly adds as Cam passes her a drink.

"Maybe Al knows someone," Cam suggests.

"Al? As in our landlord?" I say with a laugh.

They both look at me deadpan and I press my lips together because I think they are serious. But how can they be? Al is like eighty. He can't possibly know that many younger guys. I mean, he's sweet and all, but I think these two ladies are delusional.

"Yeah. Al knows everyone. Like seriously, you'd be hard-pressed to find someone in the two blocks surrounding our building who doesn't know Al. He's an absolute legend," Cam says with a shrug. "Too bad he's so old," she adds with a laugh.

We all giggle at that.

"OK, if you say so," I state.

"We do. Trust us on this one," Cam says. "Also, us ladies

like to have wine nights at Margie and Cornelia's on Tuesdays if you're interested. We meet at eight. Maybe we can even talk books again. That was fun at happy hour."

"Thanks. I'll try to make it," I say as I head back over to the shop. I'm halfway across the street when I look up to see those aqua-blue eyes looking down at me. I give a small wave, but he just closes the curtains. What the fuck is his issue?

With a sigh, I open my door and hand Jocelyn her coffee and pastry.

"What's that look for?" she asks with a raised eyebrow as she starts to put the cowboy romance books on shelves.

"Well, Carly and Cam want Al to set me up with someone. They tried to sell me on dating a guy in the building, as if. And I just got the evil eye from Mr. Grumpypants above us as I walked over here. I seriously do not get what his problem is. I just hope he's not going to be a big thorn in my side," I say with exasperation.

"It'll be fine. And isn't Al the old guy who owns this build-ing?" Jocelyn asks.

I nod as I pass her some books.

"Why not ask him to set you up? I mean, I have this friend, Alia, and her grandmother set her up and she married the guy. So you never know," Jocelyn says as she takes another handful of books from me.

"I guess so. I just want to find a good guy. Why does that seem so hard?" I open another box and Jocelyn shrugs at my question.

"It's not so much finding a good guy, it's more like finding the right one for you," she states.

I glare at her and then laugh. "Stop being so smart. Your boss doesn't like it."

She chuckles and holds up a book. "Maybe I've read too many of these books."

"Or maybe, you're just right about that." I just wish finding the right one was easier. There's an entire city of men out there. It's not like the right one is going to just walk into my store.

CHAPTER SIX

Grayson

With a long sigh, I knock on the door to...I read the newly painted sign.

Happily Ever Afters Romance Bookstore

The paper-covered door opens. My eyes widen as I take in...shit, it's starting to look like a real bookstore.

"Hey," I say as I rub my forehead.

Roxy crosses her arms and juts out a hip, flicking a hand in an "out with it" motion.

Taking another long deep breath, I study her. She's got that thick blonde hair up in some messy bun on her head. She's wearing an oversized T-shirt with leggings and she's... barefoot. That's interesting. Her toenails are painted bright red with white polka dots.

"Any chance you can stop hammering for like an hour?" I ask.

She rolls her eyes. "Yeah." She turns her head. "Jocelyn,

can you stop hanging the art? My *neighbor* is apparently trying to do something and we're annoying his life."

I glare at her. "Seriously?"

She raises an eyebrow as if to challenge me.

I glare harder. Two can play at this game.

"Thank you," I manage through gritted teeth and a clenched jaw.

"You're welcome," she says giving me a giant fake smile and then closing the door in my face.

I shake my head and run a hand over my face as I turn to go back inside.

"Rough day?" Hutch's voice calls out. I stop moving and turn to see my friend walking my way with a cup of coffee in his hand.

"Something like that. The producer asked for some different takes to the demo I sent over, but *someone*"—I nod at the bookstore—"decided to hammer artwork this morning."

He laughs as he unlocks the door and motions for me to go ahead of him. "Dude, she does have to open her shop. I'm sure she's hella stressed. I think her soft opening is in another week or two. Or at least that's what Carly and Cam were just talking about." He raises his cup of coffee as if in explanation of where he's been.

"Well, I get it, but I have work to do too," I huff as I turn and head up the stairs with Hutch in tow.

"I know. I'm just saying, you may need to compromise a little," he urges. I hate that he's right. Like a petulant child, I don't want compromise, I want what I want. I groan because even I think I sound like a dick now.

"I hate that you're right," I grumble as I unlock my door.

He chuckles and unlocks his. "Don't kill the messenger. I want both of you to succeed."

And with that, he shuts his door, and I go to walk inside

only to hear Al call out my name. He's walking down the stairs slowly. I turn and wait for him to finish the last flight.

"Good morning, Gray," he says.

"Morning, Al," I reply as I lean on my doorjamb and cross my arms. "How are you?"

"Not bad for an old man," he jokes as he gives himself a moment to catch his breath at the landing.

"You still want me to find you a date?" he asks.

I laugh. "Al, it's cool. You don't have to. I'll just ask Hutch or someone to see if they have a friend I can...uh, borrow."

He chuckles. "Borrow?"

I feel my face redden. I hate that I feel silly. I hate that he's seeing the not-so-perfect part of me. I look up to Al. He offered up this place to me when I had nowhere else to go. He may be an old family friend, but he's become more like family than any of my blood relatives. He cares and he's always showing it. He's also the closest thing I have to my grandfather who passed away about six years ago. He and Al used to play poker every week, along with several other older gentlemen. Al stopped going to the poker games when my grandfather died. He said it wasn't the same without him.

I shrug. "Something like that."

"What do you want in a woman?" he asks like he's some sort of professional matchmaker.

I raise my eyebrows. "I don't need a *real* girlfriend. I'm too busy for that right now." And I don't trust women, not after my ex dumped me for not being rich enough. It's been months, but it still stings. I thought she was the one. I loved her.

"I'm not asking if you need one. I'm asking what the perfect one would be like," he says. I look around us and quickly usher him inside. My recording can wait five minutes. Hell, for Al, it could wait all day.

I hold up a pitcher of water and he nods. I pour us both some and we sit at my dining room table.

"Trustworthy," I state.

"OK. What else? I mean, if you had to draw her up from scratch. If the universe said here, create exactly what you want..." He trails off as he watches me.

I clear my throat. I guess we're doing this.

"Trustworthy, kind, smart, funny, but in a sarcastic way, loves music, attractive." I pause as he raises a hand.

"What do you consider attractive?"

I draw a ring around a watermark on my cherrywood tabletop. Stupid Hutch left his glass here all night a few months ago and I haven't been able to get the mark to go away.

"I mean, I don't care if she has blonde hair or brown hair. I..." Shit, what do I want? I haven't thought about this in ages. "I want someone who can get dressed up and look classy, and elegant, but also doesn't care. I don't want a woman who wears eight pounds of makeup just to go grab a coffee. I like a woman with what's that little part here?" I point to the top of my lips where it makes sort of a "v" under my nose.

"You like a cupid's bow–shaped upper lip?" he asks. I want to ask why he knows this, but I decide some things are better left unsaid.

"Uh, yeah," I reply as I rub the back of my head.

"Anything else?"

I have no idea what to say to Al. It's not like there's a factory making girlfriends, at least not that I know of. I can't request my perfect girlfriend because perfect humans don't exist. Shit, look at me. I'm anything but perfect.

"No. I can't think of anything." I pause because there is one thing. Seeing Roxy with her high ponytails or buns has made me realize that I find that really attractive. It's weird. My ex never wore her hair like that.

"Out with it, kid," Al urges as he studies me.

"I like women who wear their hair up in a ponytail or bun. I mean, not like all the time, but sometimes," I mumble as I try to rationalize why I am vocalizing these words. I sound like an idiot.

"Got it. OK, I think that's enough to work with. I'll find you a date. When was this party, again?"

I don't even need to pull out my phone to check the party details. I've been worrying about it for days now. Pierce Pointer had emailed me with the details for the film's post-filming party. It was in two more days at a bar not far from here. I should have called Pierce then. I should have told him the truth or at least lied and said my ex and I broke up, which isn't a total lie, we did break up, months ago.

I hold out my phone and show him the calendar.

"I'll find you a date before then," he assures me.

"Al, I can seriously just ask a friend or something," I say as I think of Cam or Carly. As if reading my mind, he laughs.

"Ava has ballet practice that night, so Carly won't be available. And Cam is meeting with the owner of her bakery to talk about buying out the business," he says.

And there goes my two most likely dates. I fucking hate this. Why did I have to lie? What the hell is wrong with me?

Al pats my shoulder as he walks to the door. "Gray, it'll be fine. We all fuck up once in a while. You just need to see this through. You can always fake a breakup later. It's Hollywood. Those things happen all the time. And plus, you need to start dating again. And this is the perfect excuse."

I give him a deadpan stare. "Al, this wouldn't be a real date. Remember, fake date."

He waves a hand at me. "Sure thing. Fake date. It'll be like practice for a very overdue real one."

I roll my eyes. "Right."

He opens the door and turns back to me. "You know, I met Edith on a blind date."

I look over at him. He has a ghost of a smile on his lips. "She walked into the restaurant in a red dress, and I knew then that I could never let a woman that gorgeous get away or I'd regret it for the rest of my life. Then, we spent the whole night talking, and by the end of the date, I knew she was the one."

"You're a lucky man, Al." I pause and then add, "To have known a love like that...it's special. Not everyone gets to experience that."

He nods. "I know. I miss her every day."

I give him a sad smile. "We all do," I state because it's true. Edith was a great lady and everyone in this building misses her warm smiles, bear hugs, and apple strudel on Sundays.

"See you, Al," I add as he opens the door and leaves me alone with my thoughts, which are a melting pot of high ponytails, fake romances, and blind dates. Even my music doesn't push them away. Instead, I lean into them and use my instruments to pour my feelings out into the universe, as if I'm some sort of Pied Piper that can call the perfect woman with my musical notes.

CHAPTER SEVEN

Roxy

I put my hands on my hips and swivel. A smile threatens to form on my face as I look at my bookstore. It's actually looking like a bookstore. I have a tablet set up for payment. There are books on the shelves. Tables sit throughout the store with more books, T-shirts, bookmarks, stickers, and other merchandise. The pale pink walls, antique chandeliers, and floral theme make my threatening smile emerge despite all my jitters about my upcoming soft opening.

"It looks great," Jocelyn says from beside me as she stands up next to the bookshelf she was organizing.

"It does. We just need to finish the reading nook, the book club area, and that selfie area," I state as I mentally tick off items in my head.

"Sooo..." Jocelyn says as she follows my gaze around the room. "Are we still planning a soft opening for a week from Monday?"

I nod slowly because it feels like pulling off a bandage on a wound that may or may not be completely healed. I've dreamed of this for years. My obsession with romance books started when I was fifteen and spent two weeks at my grandmother's house. I found her old romance books and devoured them. Then, I'd sneak off to the bookstore or the library and find more. My siblings are all overachievers. I was not. So while they were winning awards and sports games, I was curled up with my books. It sort of became my entire personality. While my brother and sisters began doing amazing things with their adult lives, I floundered. Sure, I went to college, but then I couldn't figure out what to do. I felt paralyzed. I took odd jobs that paid minimum wage. I dated all the wrong men for all the wrong reasons. And the final blow was when my ex cheated on me. I knew my life trajectory was going in the wrong direction as I had loaded my boxes into my car following our breakup and then into my old childhood bedroom. There was no way I wanted to continue down this path, but I felt stuck.

Until my grandmother died. God, that was awful. But somehow, through all of it, I survived.

And then I learned about my inheritance. It was way more than I ever thought possible. And so, I started to dream big. Hell, I started to dream period. I hadn't done that in years. One night while going through a box of books, I had this idea. It was only an idea, but soon it grew bigger like a flame being stoked. I had no clue if I could pull it off, but here I am. Standing inside my dream next to *my* employee. Holy shitballs! I did it. I just hope I can make it work. I'm not sure I can survive my dream being crushed.

"Yep. It's time to double up on our social media posts. I'm not changing the date now. We're doing this," I state as there's a knock at the door.

Walking over to it, I open the door to find Al standing there.

He looks past me and smiles. "Edith, my wife, would love this. It's beautiful," he says before focusing back on me. He had mentioned her before and I learned that it was her antique store that was in here before I leased the space. It makes my heart hurt for Al. And it makes me feel silly for being upset about my cheating ex when Al has lost the love of his life.

I blush. "Thanks, Al. It's coming together," I reply as I smile at him.

"Well, it looks great. Are you still opening in another week or so?" he asks.

"Yep. Our soft launch is a week from Monday. I'll send out emails tomorrow." I curse myself for not sending them last week, but it's been crazy and most of the people I'm inviting already know the soft opening date.

"I'll make sure to be here," he says. We're both quiet for a beat and I wonder if he just stopped by to check on the store.

"I have a favor to ask," he says, breaking the silence.

"Oh?" I ask as my brows furrow in confusion. What favor could he possibly have?

"I overheard you telling Carly you were looking to date," he starts. OK, where the hell is this going? "I have a friend who needs a date to a party but doesn't know anyone who can attend with him. Would you be interested in going on a blind date?"

I've never been on a blind date. My entire dating life has been swiping right or being matched on some app on my phone and then hesitantly messaging the person until one of us asks to meet in person in a public venue. Shit, that doesn't sound very romantic when I think of it like that.

"I...uh, who is it?" I ask.

He blinks at me as if he hasn't heard, and just when I go ask again, he speaks. "Just a friend. He's about your age."

I want to ask why Al has friends my age, but then again,

he does seem friendly with everyone in the building, hell, in the neighborhood. Maybe it's someone who lives somewhere else on Hearts Lane?

"Just one date?" I ask.

"Just the one. I mean, unless you all want to go on another date," he stresses.

I contemplate this for a minute. Al seems like a great guy. I don't think he'd set me up with someone who was a bad person. Part of me hesitates to say yes because life is so chaotic right now, but a bigger part of me says fuck it, let's do this.

"OK," I reply slowly because I'm still not one hundred percent sure of my decision.

He smiles broadly and I see all his teeth beneath his bushy, white mustache.

"Great. I'll let him know. Now, it's Tuesday at six at this bar not far from here called Joe's Tavern. Wear a red dress, OK? And your date will have a three-piece suit with a red pocket square. He'll be at the bar."

"Uh, OK. Red dress, got it. Anything else I should know?" I ask because now I want to know everything. Like, who is this guy? What does he do for a living? Is he cute?

"Nope. That should do it," he says. He goes to leave but pauses and looks back over his shoulder at me.

"Just keep an open mind," he adds, but before I can ask why, he opens the door and leaves me standing there with more questions than answers.

I turn and look at Jocelyn, who is standing with her mouth open. "Did you just get set up on a blind date?" she asks.

I shrug. "I think so?"

"Dude, you need to use this for social media. Like seriously, have our new followers weigh in on it," she suggests. It's not a horrible idea. I've been building a few social media accounts for months now. I've had some signed book give-aways and even did a fun book box two months ago. I started having virtual monthly book club meetings after I signed the lease on the store. I don't have a ton of followers, but I have a fair amount.

So I walk over to my phone, open the video app, and press record after I sort out my hair and refresh my lipstick.

"Hey, romance readers. I have a hot question for you. Would you go on a blind date? I've just been set up on one and I need your thoughts. Drop your answers in the comments," I say before I smile and stop recording. Then I upload it to all the accounts and wait. What will people say? Are they going to think I'm an idiot?

"Let's get this wall finished," Jocelyn suggests, pulling me away from my thoughts. We work together to get a fun floral backdrop set up with a neon sign that says, Happily Ever Afters Do Come True. I set up a cute camera that prints out little photos next to it if you don't want a selfie. When we finish, I smile at the setup. It's really adorable and it looks great.

"OK, I have to admit, I love this," I say. Jocelyn nods and then frowns as she lifts her phone from her pocket.

"Uh, boss, where's your phone?" she asks.

Now, I'm frowning. Where is my phone? Oh, on the desk. I walk over and pick it up and my jaw falls open. We have hundreds of new followers, and my notifications are blowing up. I scroll through them. People are responding to my video. They are asking for details and telling me to go on the date. People are posting about their blind dates.

"Wow," I manage.

"Yeah, nice post. But you'll need more like this if we're going to get to that coveted ten-thousand-followers number," Jocelyn says.

"Shit, well, I didn't really think that would happen. But I

guess there's no turning back now," I say with a laugh, although internally I'm screaming with both terror and excitement. I'm not just putting my store out there, I'm putting myself out there. I set the phone down.

"Now what?" I ask.

"He said a red dress, right?" she asks.

I nod.

"Well, then, I think we need to go red dress shopping. And your new followers can weigh in on the dress options."

"But what does that have to do with books?" I ask.

She frowns and then runs to a few shelves and pulls off books, setting them down in front of me. They are all covers where the female lead is wearing a red dress. "You can hold up books while trying on dresses and then ask if you should be more like..." She pauses and reads the blurb on the back. "Camila or..." She looks at another book. "Ashley."

"I sort of love that idea," I grumble.

She laughs. "Damn, don't be so excited."

I giggle. "Sorry, that's bitchy of me. I just wish I could come up with ideas like that."

"Well, your great idea was hiring me," she says as she points to herself.

"Yeah, that was a pretty great idea," I agree. "Now, let's go dress shopping," I add.

She looks around us. "Now? Like, right now? But we aren't done yet."

I wave a hand. "We can finish tomorrow." Right now, I need a hot dress for this mystery date. Who knows? Maybe my follower flowersforever111 is right. They wrote: I met the love of my life on a blind date. You never know.

That's true. I never know. But I'm definitely about to find out.

CHAPTER EIGHT

Grayson

I pull on my T-shirt and put my earbuds in. I make it down to the park in record time. I crank up my music and run the five-mile trail which makes a loop back to the original pathway that starts at the end of Hearts Lane. It's a movement to my left that draws my attention. I slow down and remove my earbuds.

"Hutch?" I ask as I look at my friend and neighbor in full camo sitting in some bushes.

"Hey," he says, keeping his eyes focused on something in front of him.

I follow his gaze. The bench. No flowers yet, but it's very early, just before sunrise.

"Dude, how long have you been out here?"

"Six hours," he grunts as he chews on gum.

"Six hours! That's crazy."

He shrugs. "I'm going to figure it out. Someone has to do it. Those flowers do not magically appear."

I look around us. "Don't you have, like, work or something?"

"Yeah, in an hour," he replies, not bothering to look my way.

I study him for a long moment. Has my friend lost his ever-fucking mind? Seriously? I know it's a fun little mystery, but to have all-night surveillance seems a bit extreme.

"I bet Brayden that I can catch who does it," he says, not taking his eyes off the bench.

"How much did you bet?" I ask.

"Four hundred."

My eyes widen. "You bet four hundred dollars?"

"Did I stutter?" he asks.

"OK, well, best of luck," I add as I go to head back to the apartment building.

My phone buzzes and I see a text from Margie in the group chat.

Margie: Some sketchy-looking young man is breaking into Kasen's apartment. Should I call the cops?

Before I can respond, I see Hutch looking at his phone and typing. A moment later, a message pops up.

Hutch: Margie, did he have a key or did he break down the door?

Cornelia: For the love of God. He used a key, Margie.

Margie: But why does he have a key? Maybe he stole it from Kasen's cousin.

Hutch: So...no break-in?

Me: I'll come take a look.

Hutch: I'll come with you.

I look over and Hutch gets up.

"What? Leaving your stakeout?" I pretend to be shocked.

He glares at me. "I'll just need to find another night to do it."

"Well, it's going to rain this week, so good luck."

"I won't melt, dude," he says as we walk back to the building.

Cam is coming out the door as we approach it and she gives Hutch a once-over.

"Uh, do they allow hunting in the park?" she asks with a raised eyebrow.

"No, I was watching for the flowers," he explains and starts to gesture back to the bench and stops. "You have got to be fucking kidding me."

We all turn to see flowers on the bench.

I can't help myself as I start laughing and so does Cam. She doubles over.

"Oh my God! Did you actually sit out there waiting and now they just appeared?" she manages in between fits of giggles.

"Maybe," he grumbles.

She pats his arm. "It's OK. You can try another day. Where are you two off to?"

"Margie thinks someone broke into Kasen's place, but it's probably just a friend feeding the sea creatures," Hutch explains.

"Anemones," Cam states.

"Yeah, whatever," he replies as he starts to go to the elevator.

"It's not working today," Cam calls out while crossing the street to the café.

Hutch groans and we start up the stairs. I take my shirt off after the first two flights and I wipe my face with it.

It's balmy in here today.

As we round the corner to Kasen's floor, I run smack-dab into a warm body. It takes me a millisecond to realize that my chest is flush against Roxy's. We both stare at each other like we've just run into a troll or a zombie and then we both quickly jump back.

"S-sorry," she stammers, looking everywhere but at me. Her eyes dart to my chest and then to my face. I watch the color creep across her cheeks, highlighting all those cute little freckles. Cute? Huh. Not going to unpack that thought.

"It's cool. Hutch, anything?" I call out as I step around her.

"Nope. Everything seems fine. The door is locked. No signs of forced entry. I'm sure it was just someone checking on those animals," he says.

"Animals?" Roxy's voice calls out from behind me.

"Oh, hey, Roxy. Kasen has...what are they called again?" he asks me.

I sigh. "Sea anemones."

"Interesting," she mumbles.

The door flies open to Margie and Cornelia's apartment.

"Was it a break-in?" Margie asks.

I shake my head. "Nope. Probably just checking on the sea anemones."

Cornelia swats at her friend. "I told you. You're so paranoid."

"Well, we're old ladies. What if that young man wanted to...you know?" she says.

Hutch presses his lips together to keep from laughing. I nudge him in the ribs because Margie is serious.

Roxy steps beside me. "You ladies just call me if you need anything. I'll be downstairs all day. I'll keep an eye out front for you."

"Thank you, dear," Margie says as she shuts her door. We can hear the two of them continuing to bicker through the metal barrier.

Roxy looks at both of us. "I have questions," she asks.

"Hutch was trying to catch the flower gifter," I explain.

She frowns and Hutch shrugs. "I would have been able to

if it weren't for those pesky kids," he says, pointing to Margie and Cornelia's apartment.

I start laughing as does Roxy. "Well, Scooby Doo, I do hope you can solve your mystery another day."

"Oh, I will. Rest assured," Hutch promises as he walks around us and starts down the stairs.

"What are you doing here?" I ask Roxy, eyeing her suspiciously.

"Al made me another key," she explains as she holds up a single metal key.

Then she leans in toward me. "Or maybe, I was breaking into apartments," she teases with a wink and spins on her heel heading downstairs.

I take a deep breath and shake my head. What a strange start to my day. I hope the party later will be full of fewer surprises.

———

"Good to see you," Pierce says. An attractive woman with dark hair and dark eyes accompanies him. I shake his hand.

"This is my wife, Haven," he adds.

I shake her hand next. "It's a pleasure to meet you, Haven."

"Likewise," she replies with a warm smile.

Pierce looks around me. "Where's your girlfriend?"

I swallow hard. I hate lying. "Uh, she's coming from work. Should be here soon," I manage. I am so fucked. Why the hell am I still lying?

"Great. I look forward to meeting her. I love those changes you sent over, by the way," he says as he reaches for a flute of champagne on a tray held by a passing waiter. He hands it to his wife and I see her hand that's wrapped through his arm grip him a little tighter.

"Thanks. I appreciate that," I say.

"We can talk shop later. Enjoy yourself. Wade is around here somewhere, and you met Martin already, right?" he asks, mentioning the director as he walks off toward someone who's waving at him. Haven gives me a small smile and nods and I return them.

I sit back down and sip my gin. Where is this mystery woman? Al assured me she'd be here promptly at six. I check my watch again. It's a pricey Rolex my parents gave me for Christmas five years ago, back when we used to talk more often than just big family parties and events. I wouldn't say I'm estranged from them, but I'm definitely on their shit list.

A movement to my right draws my attention from my drink. My eyes connect with long, shapely legs in high heels, then a red dress that hugs curves that have my dick already perking up, and then a low v-cut neckline that flaunts some gorgeous breasts, and it's as my gaze continues up to her face that I see it's...Roxy. Wait a damn minute. There's no fucking way.

Nope. No. Al would not do me dirty like this. He knows I'm annoyed with Roxy for making so much noise. Why would he think this was a good idea? Fuck my life.

Roxy's eyes widen as her gaze meets mine. Her step falters for a second about ten steps from me. We both stare at each other for what seems like an eternity.

"Is this your girlfriend?" Pierce's voice comes from behind me. Roxy's eyes follow the sound of the voice and then land back on me. She looks pissed. Fuck. This is going to be bad. So bad.

CHAPTER NINE

Roxy

I can practically feel the nervous energy vibrating off Grayson. Fuck. What in the hell was Al thinking? He knows Grayson detests me...and my store. Shit. I shouldn't have agreed to this. Why didn't I ask who the guy was? God, I'm so stupid.

Grayson's Adam's apple bobs as he swallows. His eyes penetrate mine. Damn, he's silently pleading with me. Fuck. I'm such a damn sucker. Even if he's a total jerk, I can't do this to him. I've heard for weeks now from everyone in the building about Grayson's big chance. I know he had a post-filming party to attend this week. And looking around, this has to be it. I do not want to be the reason he loses it. I don't need guilt added to my already broken self-confidence.

"Yes, hi. I'm Roxy Benedict. Nice to meet you," I say as I extend my hand, trying to pull myself together and pretend to be...Grayson's girlfriend, date, who knows?

"Pierce Pointer," he says. "And this is my wife, Haven." A

stunning woman by his side holds out her hand and I shake it. He looks vaguely family and so does his wife. I've probably seen them online somewhere. I make a mental note to do an Internet search later.

"Nice to meet you both," I say as I lean against Grayson. He tentatively wraps an arm around my waist.

"Hey," he says, his voice low and gruff. What in the hell? Grayson has a sexy public voice. I did not see that coming.

"Hey, sorry I'm late," I say as I lean up on my tiptoes and give his cheek a quick peck.

"No worries, baby. Everything OK?" he asks.

"Yep, just taking care of something at the store," I explain because that's actually the truth and you're supposed to stick to truths in these situations. Or at least I think that's what I should do.

"Oh? You have a store?" Haven asks.

I nod. "A romance bookstore. Over on Hearts Lane."

She claps her hands together. "OMG! I love romance books. You'll have to give me some recommendations."

"Of course." I nod and smile.

A man calls out to Pierce, and he turns and waves. "I'm sorry. It's an old friend of ours. Will you please excuse us? It was great meeting you, Roxy. Hopefully, we'll have more time to chat soon," Pierce says.

"Sure thing," I say with a smile. They walk away and I step back and turn to Grayson. "What the fuck is going on?" I hiss as I feel daggers shooting from my eyes to his.

He sighs and puts a finger up to the bartender who nods and pours more gin into Grayson's glass.

"And...what would you like?" Grayson asks. I don't answer. "Give us just a minute," he tells the bartender who mutters, "OK" and walks away, tossing a towel onto his shoulder.

"I bailed your ass out. I'm leaving. You can tell Pierce we had a fight or something," I mutter as I turn to leave. A hand grabs my wrist and I pause, spinning back around on my stiletto heels.

"Please stay, just for one drink. I feel bad. I didn't know Al was...I didn't know," Grayson pleads. His eyes search mine and for reasons unknown to my conscious, I agree.

"Fine. One drink," I state. "But only because I'm all dressed up, so I might as well enjoy a..." I look up at the board. "A kir royale."

"One kir royale," Grayson says to the bartender before turning back to me.

"I..." I look around us suddenly feeling super awkward. "I'm just going to run to the bathroom. I'll be right back."

I scurry away before he can answer me and head toward the back of the bar, which is where I assume they are. I breathe a sigh of relief when I see the restroom sign with an arrow. Weaving around partygoers, I make my way there. Under normal circumstances, I'd be looking for celebrities and excited that I'm at a Hollywood party, but today, I'm just annoyed. I find one of the unisex single-person bathrooms unoccupied, and I step inside and lock the door behind me.

I press my back against it and pull my phone out of my small purse. I have no idea why, but I call Jocelyn because my siblings won't understand, Tay is too many time zones ahead to be awake, and Carly and Cam are clearly on team Grayson.

"Roxy?" she answers, her voice filled with confusion. "I thought you had the big date tonight."

"I do," I whisper.

"Why are we whispering?" she asks in a whisper.

I groan. "I don't know. I'm in the bathroom."

"Is it that bad?" she asks.

"Worse," I reply as I push off the door and walk in front of the mirror. I look good. Which now seems like such a waste of makeup and hair product.

"Does he have bad hair? Oh, wait, he's like catfishing you. Is he seventy with missing teeth?" Jocelyn asks.

"It's a blind date. How could he be catfishing me?" I ask with a frown as I set my purse down and pull out my red lipstick.

"OK, so what's wrong?" she asks.

"It's Grayson."

There's no response. The line is silent. I pull the phone away from my face and look down at it. "Jocelyn?"

"Yeah. I'm here. Just...processing. So, is this a hard-pass situation? Like, you could never date Grayson?" she asks.

"I mean...he's my neighbor...and he sort of doesn't like me," I stammer as I try to explain myself.

"One, he's your hot neighbor. And two, he doesn't like noise. He never said he doesn't like *you*," she points out and I hate that she's right.

"Yeah. OK. But he's so...just...you know," I try to find the words, but I'm failing epically.

"Just give him a chance. You never know. Plus, this will make for amazing social media fodder. Like seriously, do it for the followers," she says, her voice rising on the last statement.

"I don't know," I say as I chew on my lower lip. I don't want to make things worse between Grayson and me. "I don't really think it's a blind date. I think he wants me to pretend to be his girlfriend. I remember Carly saying something about how he told some people he needed a fake girlfriend for this event, and then Al asks me to do him this favor by going on a blind date, and when I got here that producer came over to meet Grayson's *girlfriend*," I explain in rapid succession.

"Shit. I still say do it. You get followers, he gets a fake girl-friend...I mean, have a talk with him about this whole fake-girlfriend thing, but maybe by doing this, he'll warm up to you, and the store," she says.

I stop chewing on my lip and stare at my reflection. "Fuck

it. OK. You aren't wrong. Maybe it will help. I mean, if I'm doing him this favor, then maybe he'll lay off us about any noise we might make."

"And for the followers," she adds.

"Yeah, yeah. That too. OK, I'm going back out there. Wish me luck," I say.

"You won't need it. That dress you found is *hot*," she says.

"Fake girlfriend," I remind her.

"Whatever you say," she says and then hangs up.

I sigh, check myself in the mirror one more time, and pull out my phone, posting a selfie and asking my followers if they knew the blind date and weren't sure if they liked the person, would they bail on the date or stay. I put my phone away and unlock the door. When I open it, I find Grayson standing against the wall. His eyes meet mine.

"Everything OK?" he asks.

I nod, hoping like hell he didn't just hear my entire conversation.

He runs a hand through his messy dark hair, and somehow, it makes him look even hotter. So unfair.

"I'm sorry. I'm guessing Al didn't tell you anything either?" he asks.

I shake my head and he blows out a long breath.

"I may have told Pierce I had a girlfriend. And I sort of felt like an idiot because, spoiler alert, I do not have one. I couldn't bring myself to tell him. And saying I just broke up with one seems...weird. I thought Al would explain it to whoever he invited..." He trails off and I'm getting lost-boy vibes. Shit. I'm a total sucker for that. I feel myself caving further.

I hold up a hand.

"OK, here's how this is going to go. I will be your fake girlfriend. No touching beyond like a hug or something or a quick peck on the cheek. The store is opening soon, so I don't have a ton of time to just go out randomly to events, but if you give me a little notice, I will do my best to be there. We can fake date for like...a month or two and then, we fake break up, comprendé?" I state.

He tilts his head a little and I'm wondering what he's thinking. But I don't have to wait long.

"Comprendé," he says. "But what's in it for you?" he asks.

"Not sure yet, but you can't be too mad at your fake girl-friend if her store is noisy, can you?" I ask with a pointed look.

He chuckles. "I guess not."

"Well, then." I hold out my hand and he takes it in his. "We have a deal, Mr. Porter."

He steps away from the wall and offers me his arm. I loop mine through his and we make our way back to the bar where a kir royale sits waiting for me.

He pulls back a barstool and I take a seat in it. Leaning against me, he whispers in my ear, "Thank you, Roxy."

The feel of his warm breath on my earlobe gives me a shiver as I pick up the champagne flute and take a long sip of the drink. This should be interesting.

———

I bend over laughing as we approach the apartment building.

"You did not," I manage to say after I compose myself.

He smiles at me, his aqua-blue eyes twinkling. "I did so."

"And no one noticed that you put googly eyes on all the instruments?" I ask incredulously.

Shaking his head, he gives me another boyish grin.

"Wow. That's hilarious," I state. We walk a few paces in silence. I did not think my evening would be this fun. Gray, as he insisted I call him, is actually really nice. I admit, I had a little whiplash when I realized he wasn't a monster, but I'm getting used to this side of him. We left the party around eleven and grabbed a drink at another bar before heading back here.

"Watch out," Gray says as he takes my hand to help me over a puddle.

He doesn't let go right away and I don't pull my hand away either until we reach the apartment door.

"I...had fun tonight," he says.

I roll my eyes. "You say that like you were forced to go to a birthday party for a kid you don't like."

"Well, I admit, I didn't think I'd have fun, and honestly, I was a little worried when Al said he'd find me a date."

I give a little laugh. "Fine, I was equally concerned when Al asked me to go out on a blind date with someone."

We both stand there grinning at each other like two middle schoolers. Gray leans over and kisses my cheek and I blush.

"I had a good time with you, Roxy," he says as he pulls back.

I go to lean in and kiss him on the lips because I'm sort of drunk and he smells good, and damn, he is hot. But then, a little voice calls out from above us.

"Are you guys going to kiss like in the movies?" Ava asks.

Gray's eyes widen and I'm sure mine do too as we both look up and see Ava leaning out her window.

"Ava, be careful," Gray says, and damn it if his protectiveness over this little girl doesn't tug at my ovaries.

"Mr. Gray, I *am* being careful. I only have my head sticking out. The rest of me is on Mr. Pickles," she explains.

I press my lips together to keep from laughing but my entire body starts shaking. Gray leans down and smiles at me.

"We were just saying good night, Ava. Go back to bed or I'll have to come up there," he says.

"OK, good night," she says quickly and closes her window.

We both burst into laughter.

"Oh my God!" I say as I press a hand to my chest. "Who is Mr. Pickles?"

"Her giant stuffed donkey. Brayden got it for her when she turned three. She had a donkey obsession after visiting a petting zoo," he explains with a laugh.

"Right. Well, good night...Mr. Gray," I tease as I unlock my door and step through the threshold.

"Good night, Roxy," Gray says as he waits till the door is shut and then goes inside the apartment building. I walk to the back of my store and into my small studio, smiling while I change into my pajamas. Maybe this Tin Man has a heart after all.

CHAPTER TEN

Grayson

I sit at the bar. Al is shaking a martini and talking to Carly. Ava is sitting next to Brayden, sipping a Shirley Temple. And Cam and Drew are standing at the end of the bar arguing over who is better at blowjobs, only they are using code words in front of Ava.

"You know I have technique at blowing bubbles," Cam argues.

"There's no way. I've blown way more bubbles than you. It's not even a competition," Drew scoffs.

"Ladies, ladies, ladies, I'm sure you are both amazing at blowing bubbles," Hutch says as he wraps an arm around each of them and leans toward the bar. "Hey, Al, do we have any of that lager left from last week?"

"Sure do," Al says with a grin as he pours Cam her martini and then grabs a lager from the mini-fridge.

"Sweet. Thanks," Hutch says, taking his beer and walking back over to sit with Margie and Cornelia.

"I can blow really big bubbles," Ava says proudly.

Carly spits out her drink, coughing as she tries to compose herself. Brayden pats her on the back but has to turn away. Al grimaces. And Cam, Drew, and I lose it.

"What? I can. Mom, can I go get my bubble gun?" she asks innocently.

It takes a full thirty seconds for all of us to compose ourselves.

"Maybe later, sweetie. I think everyone just has some really great memories of blowing bubbles," she says, which leads to another round of laughs.

"Come on, Ava. I'll go with you. We can grab that bubble set I bought you last summer," Brayden suggests.

"Bray, it's OK," Carly protests.

He holds up a hand. "Nope, our girl here needs bubbles. It's a bubble emergency," he says as he picks Ava up and she squeals in delight. He carries her to the door, and they disappear down the steps.

"Shit! Poor Ava. I'm sorry, Carly. We should have used some other boring term instead," Cam says with a giggle.

"I'm not calling blowjobs something boring like ironing or paying taxes," Drew argues.

"Hey, sorry I'm late," Roxy's voice rings out from the door. I turn to see her walking toward us. She's wearing a sundress that hugs her curves. Damn, she's gorgeous. I'm a lucky bastard to have such a hot fake girlfriend.

"What?" she asks me as she slides onto the stool that Brayden had been occupying.

"Nothing. You look nice," I say. I'm about to say we should go out to dinner to discuss things and get our story straight when the door opens, and Ava and Brayden come back with armloads of bubble-making stuff.

"Hey, who's that guy checking on Kasen's sea anemones? It's not his cousin," he says.

"You saw that guy too? I don't recognize him. Should we call Kasen or uh, what's his cousin's name?" Cam asks.

"Uh, crazy idea here, but if he's using a key, don't we assume he's supposed to be there?" Roxy asks.

"Yes, or it could be...also, his cousin's name is Elliott," Drew trails off as he looks around at everyone, clearly trying to insinuate something dark and nefarious is happening in Kasen's apartment.

Al laughs. "Drew, you have an overactive imagination."

Cam leans toward me. "Do you think Kasen knows someone else is coming? You know how he is about his apartment."

"Kasen's fine. I got a text from him last week. He said his contract got extended and he had someone checking on things while he was gone," Al assures us.

"But he always has Elliott checking on things," Carly points out.

"Just text him. He's fine. I swear," Al reassures us. We all mumble agreements, but I can tell most of us are still unsure. Kasen's never been gone for this long and no one other than Elliott has ever come to his apartment to check on things.

I look over at Brayden and he gives me a subtle nod. Yep, we will most definitely be chatting more about this later. I pull out my phone and text Kasen.

Me: Everything OK?

There's no immediate response or three little dots—just a "delivered" below my message. Sighing, I stick my phone back in my pocket.

Roxy glances over at me. "So, uh..." She trails off and looks around us. It takes me a half second but I realize she isn't sure if we should be talking about our fake-dating thing in front of everyone. Although it's clear that Al knows and that man is watching us like a hawk.

We both turn toward him and he gives us a wink. Roxy blushes and looks down at her drink.

"How's the bookstore coming along?" I inquire because that topic seems safe. We've barely scratched the surface of knowing anything about each other.

"Good," she says as she swirls the liquid in her glass.

"You ready for your opening day?" I ask.

She turns slightly and our legs touch. She freezes as if she doesn't know if that's OK. I press my thigh against her knee and she relaxes her shoulders.

"Yes. I think so. I mean, it's a 'soft launch' day. The big 'opening day' celebration will be next month. I just want to work out all the bugs first, you know?" she explains.

Smiling, I shake my head. "Nope. But I get that. It sounds like a smart decision."

"Hey, everyone! Look at my giant bubbles! See, I told you I'm the best at blowing bubbles!" Ava screams as she runs across the rooftop deck with what looks like a Hula-Hoop-sized ring that is blowing enormous bubbles behind her as she runs.

Cam loses it, followed by Drew, and then everyone starts laughing.

Ava pauses and looks at us. "What? It's not funny. I'm good," she says, and I see the tears welling. Shit.

Brayden composes himself first and runs over to her and scoops her up, putting her on his shoulders. He bounces her a little and she giggles.

"Ava is the world champion of bubble blowing!" he says loudly.

Everyone applauds and Ava giggles some more. I glance over at Carly who is mouthing, "Thank you," to Brayden. Brayden just nods as he brings Ava toward the bar area.

"Watch your head, kiddo," he says as he ducks down.

Ava leans down and puts her head on Brayden's shoulder,

wrapping her arms tightly around his neck. He coughs and reaches up to loosen them a little.

"Don't kill Bray, Ave. He needs to breathe," Cam teases.

"Sorry, Unca Bray," Ava says and she kisses his cheek and squeezes harder hugging him. Secretly, I love it when she calls him that. She couldn't say his name or mister when she was three. So he tried to teach her to say Uncle Bray and that didn't go as planned either. For some reason, the nickname just stuck. She loosens her arms and rests her head again on his shoulder. Fuck. That kid is adorable.

I look back over at Roxy who is watching Ava and Brayden. I need to get her alone for a few minutes so we can chat.

"Hey, you want to go on a mission to check out Kasen's place? I have a spare key for emergencies," I state.

Everyone turns to me.

"You do?" Cam asks.

"Uh, yeah. So does Al and so does Troy," I say with a laugh.

"Oh. Why doesn't Kasen just have you check in on his apartment?" Drew asks with a raised eyebrow.

"'Cause I suck at sea creatures," I explain.

Troy walks over and starts laughing. "He did once, and then he had a lot less animals afterward," he says.

I frown. "I mean, yeah, that happened. But he didn't even ask you or Al," I point out.

"He didn't ask me because Edith told him all about how I killed a bunch of her fish. And Troy flat-out refused to take responsibility," Al says.

"Wait. You killed Kasen's sea anemones?" Roxy asks. Then she frowns. "I don't even know if I've ever seen one. Maybe at an aquarium?"

I take her arm. "Come on. I'll text him we are checking to make sure a leak didn't impact his apartment while Troy is fixing it."

"So, you're gonna lie to your friend," she says with a raised eyebrow.

"I'll come too. I got to see this," Hutch says from behind me. Shit. Fucking Hutch, ruining my plan.

I reach for my phone and add a message to my text chat with Kasen and then walk down to my apartment and grab the key. Hutch and Roxy are waiting by Kasen's door when I get there.

"OK, just act normal. Remember, there's a *leak*," I say.

"Why do we have to act *normal*?" Roxy asks.

Hutch starts laughing and so do I. "Uh, Kasen has cameras. He's very big on security."

"So, why are we concerned, then? Wouldn't he just check his cameras and see if something was going on?" she asks, her brows furrowed with confusion. Fuck. She looks adorable when she doesn't understand something. Her whole face is pinched in concentration as she tries to figure out what's happening.

"Kasen doesn't have cameras everywhere. It's just to check on the tank. And he can see the door, but if he's really busy and knows someone is coming by, he could miss it," Hutch explains.

"OK, remember, we're checking for a leak. And then keep an eye out for anything amiss," I state as I unlock his door.

Roxy and Hutch nod as I open the door. I punch a code into his alarm, hoping he hasn't changed it. It disarms and Roxy gasps as she looks at the enormous tank along the far wall of the living room. She slowly walks over and examines it. The tank has some corals and a few little fish, but it's the half dozen sea anemones that pique her interest. I watch as she leans forward to examine them.

I lean down next to her and she jumps and clutches her chest.

"Christ! Don't scare me like that," she breathes.

I put a hand on her back as she stands, guiding her toward the kitchen.

"The leak could be in here. Let's make sure. Hutch, check the bathrooms, please," I say. Once we are clear of Hutch, I lean forward. "Let's go out tomorrow night and discuss things," I say in a low voice.

"OK. It'll have to be later," she whispers and looks past my shoulder. I glance behind me, but Hutch isn't there yet.

"That's fine. Text me when you're available and I'll send you an address of a bar. It's a few streets over, but no one from here goes there. They don't like the drink menu," I explain.

She gives me a pointed look. "So why are *we* going there?"

"Because we won't be caught. Unless you want to tell everyone." I motion toward Hutch.

She shrugs. "OK. I...let's discuss it then. I hadn't really thought about what we tell other people." She hadn't? I'm an idiot. Of course, she hadn't. Why would she? She's starting to get to know everyone here. I don't like keeping things from my friends, but I also am afraid of what they'll say if they know. It's bad enough that Al knows. Everyone knowing would make all of this ten times more awkward.

"Guys? If Kasen is abroad, why is his passport sitting here on his dresser?" Hutch's voice calls out from the bedroom, interrupting our conversation.

We both turn and head toward Hutch.

He's holding a passport open to Kasen's face.

I take it from him and frown. "That's strange. Maybe he forgot it?"

Hutch gives me a pointed look. "Right. Because he could totally get into another country legally without a passport."

Roxy shrugs. "Maybe he's not in another country."

"Come on. I don't see anything else. And if he's texted Al, then we at least know he's OK," I say as I usher them both to the front door. I look around once more and see nothing out of place. Hopefully, Kasen will get back to me and everyone can get back to focusing on the mystery of the bench flowers instead of Kasen's whereabouts.

I follow Roxy up the stairs, watching her ass sway with each step. This woman has surprised the hell out of me. I didn't think I'd like her, but now, I sort of wish I could take her on a real date because the more I get to know her, the more I realize I do like her. I hope this fake-dating thing doesn't fuck things up between us. Part of me wishes I could tell everyone and get their advice. Keeping this a secret is going to be a nightmare.

CHAPTER ELEVEN

Roxy

"His passport is still there," Hutch announces as we exit the stairwell.

"Say what? I thought he was abroad, like in Sweden or Italy or something," Drew says. I walk through the door and find everyone looking toward us with their mouths gaping. Even Al looks a little surprised.

Gray comes up behind me. I feel the heat of his body against my back, and for reasons I can't explain, goose bumps form on my arms. I rub them and step to the side, not wanting to explore why I was loving him there.

"First off, Drew, those aren't even near each other. Secondly, Al, I thought you said he was abroad for his contract work," Gray states, his arm brushing mine. I feel like a schoolgirl with a crush. I want him to touch me. Fuck, I'm being ridiculous. Gray is just my neighbor and my *fake boyfriend*. Nothing more is going to come of that.

"That's it. We need a s'mores night. I'm texting Kasen

again," Gray adds as he walks over to the bar. I follow him, leaning toward Hutch as I walk. Ava cheers and Cam gives her a high five.

"What's a s'mores night?" I whisper.

Hutch chuckles and wraps a giant arm around my shoulder. "Well, some nights, our happy hour goes a little late. We turn on the fire pit and make s'mores. If you're lucky, we can get Gray to play us some music."

"I'll get out the s'mores stuff," Al says.

"I'll grab my cello," Gray offers as he turns back toward the door.

"Wow, live music and chocolate. This place is way better than Al described," I joke.

Cam smiles. "It's the best."

"I'll get the fire going. Anyone want the hot tub tonight?" Troy asks as he walks over to the fire pit.

"Me!" Ava squeals.

"Ava, you can make one s'more. But then we have to go to bed. You have school tomorrow. Remember?" Carly says.

"But, Mom!" Ava protests as everyone chuckles.

Carly sighs.

"How about you and me and your mom have another s'more night this weekend?" Brayden asks.

"Really?" Ava replies. "You promise!"

"Pinky promise," he says with a grin and holds up his pinky finger. She wraps her little pinky around his and her smile radiates up at him like he's the center of her universe.

"Don't forget about us. We'll come up here for more hot tub time too," Margie calls out from the chairs where she sits with Jessa and Cornelia.

Everyone chuckles.

Al comes back with the s'mores supplies and Grayson follows a few minutes later with his cello. The sky is darkening and Cam and Drew sink into the jacuzzi while having a debate about Kasen's whereabouts. A few others chime in with ideas. Hutch pats the seat next to him and we each put a marshmallow on sticks. I twirl mine until it's golden brown.

Grayson sits on a bench and begins to play a classical piece of music. I think it's Beethoven or Mozart. I'm not sure, but it's beautiful. A calm quiet descends on everyone as we listen to the melody. I study Gray as he plays. His eyes close and his body seems as in tune to the instrument as his mind. His fingers press down on the strings and draw the bow back and forth over them. He sways a little with each note as if he feels it in his soul. It's mesmerizing to watch. I make my s'more, keeping my eyes on him. I groan a little as I taste the chocolate and Gray's eyes open, meeting mine. He watches me intently as I lick some chocolate from my finger. I make way more of a show of licking it off than I should because, for some reason, I want to tease this man.

His gaze seems to penetrate mine, and I notice him smirking. Jackass. He knows exactly what I'm doing.

I look away, ending our little battle of staring.

"OK, last s'more, kiddo. Say good night to everyone," Carly says to Ava as Ava finishes her creation which includes sprinkles that Al had up at the bar. Ava called them unicorn desserts, which made everyone laugh.

"'Night," she says on a yawn.

"I got her," Brayden says as he picks up a very sleepy Ava. Carly trails behind them giving everyone a wave.

I lean over to Drew because I feel like Drew and Cam know all the building gossip. "Is there something between Carly and Brayden?"

Drew laughs. "Uh, no. Those two are oblivious to the chemistry between them. They've been thick as thieves since Carly moved in here a few years ago. And I've never seen either one make a move for the other." He shrugs.

"Hey, Gray, play the theme song from *Titanic*!" Cam shouts out.

Gray groans. "Seriously, Cam? You always request that."

"It sounds so good on the cello, please?" she asks, drawing out the last word.

He rolls his eyes but complies. She claps her hands excitedly and leans over Drew. "He's so good, right?"

I nod. Because he is good. He mentioned that he studied music in college, but worked in his family business until two years ago. I wonder what made him decide to do music full-time. The thought nags at me as I continue to listen.

Gray finishes and sets down his instrument. "Hand me a marshmallow," he asks Hutch. Hutch tosses him the bag.

I watch as he burns a marshmallow to a crisp and makes a s'more. "Is there anything left of that marshmallow besides char?" I tease.

"Don't knock it till you try it," he retorts as he takes a bite.

I put one last marshmallow on my stick and carefully rotate it. I place it on the graham cracker over exactly four squares of chocolate and then finish with a second graham cracker half. I take a bite and close my eyes as I relish the taste of the warmed chocolate.

When I open my eyes again, I find Gray watching me.

"What?" I manage after I swallow my bite.

"You have a little chocolate..." He trails off but motions by my lower lip.

I wipe it and he shakes his head. Reaching over he swipes a finger along my lip before he pulls it away and licks the chocolate from his skin.

Our eyes stay locked. Why do I feel like that's the hottest thing I've ever seen?

Al comes around with hot chocolates and various alcohols to put in them. I take Baileys in mine.

Leaning back, I look up at the stars. I can't see many here with all the city lights, but I can see some.

"Do you ever miss seeing them?" I ask no one in particular.

"Seeing what?" Gray questions. I glance over at him. He's sitting on the outdoor sectional perpendicular to the part I'm on. I scoot into the corner and point to the sky.

"The stars," I say.

"Good night, we're off to bed," Jessa and Troy say in unison, interrupting various conversations.

"Us too," Margie and Cornelia chime in together.

One by one, folks begin to say goodbyes until it's just Gray, Cam, Drew, Hutch, Al, and me. Cam and Drew are back to their discussion about Kasen's whereabouts. Hutch and Al are discussing the local football team while attempting to chime in on Kasen, but it's clear Al isn't worried and Hutch isn't sure what to think. And Gray and I are left alone in the corner of the sectional.

We're quiet for a few minutes.

"I do miss them," Gray finally answers the question. "My family has a lake house and my sister and I would sit out on our dock and look at the stars for hours."

"You have a sister?" I ask, turning my head to look at his profile. He keeps his gaze above us.

"I do. Younger by four years," he states. "You?"

"I have an older sister, a younger brother, and a younger sister."

He turns his head. "That's a lot of kids."

Giggling, I keep my gaze on his. "It's only four, not fourteen. Plus, Isla was a bit of a surprise."

He grins. "She's the one that was helping you at your store, right?"

I nod, impressed he remembered that.

"They must be proud of you," he says as he searches my eyes.

"I guess so. I mean, they are all really successful, so...I'm not sure opening a bookstore falls into the impressive category."

"What? Why not?" he asks, turning more toward me.

"Well, my older sister, Cybil, lives in New York City and is a professor of law. My brother, Jasper, is in IT and owns his own company. And Isla is in grad school for psychology. They are all overachievers, and then, there's me," I explain.

"You're what, twenty-something. And you're opening a bookstore. How is that not impressive?" he questions.

Shrugging, I answer, "Because it's just a bookstore and I only can afford to do it because I inherited money when our grandmother passed away. It's not like I worked for it. I'm not curing cancer of something important."

Gray gets a look that I can't quite decipher, anger, annoyance. I can't tell. "It's impressive, Roxy. Very impressive."

He reaches over and gently lifts a lock of hair away from my eye. I freeze. We're so close I can smell the hot chocolate on his breath and feel the heat of his skin. I start to lean forward toward his lips. He doesn't turn away. Just as I'm an inch away, Drew yawns loudly.

"I need sleep, people," he says loudly and stands. I jump back from Gray who has an amused look on his face. What the fuck? What is that about?

I stand abruptly because I need to get away from Gray. That was clearly some weird reaction to alcohol. I should go before I try to seduce my fake boyfriend.

"I'm going to head down. Al, you need help cleaning up?"

Al waves a hand at me. "Nah, it's Hutch's turn to clean up."

I giggle as Hutch groans.

"I'll walk you down," Gray says as Cam follows Drew to the door.

I follow Gray, and when we reach his apartment, I stop.

"I got it from here. I'll see you Tuesday," I state.

"I want to know you got inside," he says not budging. I glare at him. I don't know why his chivalry is annoying me, but it is. He sighs and waves a hand.

"Come here. There's a back way," he explains.

I frown but follow him. He takes me past the mail slots on the first floor, into the back hallway that leads out to our courtyard and driveway into the garage under the building. There's a little fence separating my back entrance from the garden. He pushes on it and a gate swings open.

"Huh. Al didn't show me that," I say with a frown, wondering how I haven't discovered that yet. I guess I've been too preoccupied.

"Well, he probably forgot. Good night," he says as he watches me unlock my door. "Roxy?"

I pause as I push the door open. "Yes?"

"I had fun tonight. Thanks for agreeing to fake date me," he says quietly.

I smile into the darkness of my studio. "You're welcome. Good night," I say, and I walk into my apartment and shut the door. I pull my shirt up against my nose, realizing it smells like Gray's cologne from where I was leaning my shoulder against his. Fuck, why does my fake boyfriend have to smell so damn good? And why did I almost kiss him tonight? I need to improve my fake-girlfriend skills. I absolutely cannot go falling for a man who doesn't want a real relationship. That's the last thing I need right now. Geez, I'm going to suck at being a fake girlfriend.

CHAPTER TWELVE

Grayson

I sit on my sofa, staring at the wall. What the fuck just happened? I almost kissed Roxy. I shake my head. No. It was just the alcohol. That didn't almost happen, or did it? Shit.

Sighing, I text the only person I can trust about this. Brayden. Aside from Kasen, he's the most like Fort Knox of anyone in the building.

Me: You back from Ava tuck-in duty?

Bray: Yep. What's up?

Me: I need advice.

Bray: Shit. You must be hard-pressed for it if you're asking me. Come on up.

I head to Bray's apartment, knocking on the door only once before he opens it. I walk past him and sit down on one of his two oversized leather chairs.

"I need to tell you something but you are sworn to absolute secrecy. You cannot tell Carly or anyone else," I begin.

He sits down on the other chair. "OK," he says slowly.

"Roxy is my fake girlfriend," I blurt out while staring down at the ground and running a hand through my hair. After a moment of silence, I glance over at him.

He opens his mouth, closes it, and opens it again. "I... what?" he stammers.

Sighing, I lean back in the chair and stare at his ceiling.

"I maybe fucked up and told Pierce I had a girlfriend. Then I felt stupid telling the truth, so I mentioned it to Al. Al says no worries, I'll get a woman to be your fake girlfriend." I pause as Bray laughs.

I look over at him and glare.

He puts his hands up in the air. "Sorry. My bad. It's just... you let Al set you up. That was your first mistake. He's like the fairy godfather that no one wants. His heart's in the right place, but..." I level a harder stare at him, and he trails off.

"So he says a woman will meet me at the post-filming party. And Roxy shows up. She's as shocked as I am. But agrees to do it. I think she thinks that I won't bitch about noise if we're fake dating," I say with a bitter laugh because that's never happening.

"Anyhow, we've agreed to fake date for the purposes of me keeping this contract with Pierce for the film's score."

I look back at Bray.

"So, what's the problem?" he asks.

I put my hands over my face and drag them down my skin. "I think I fucking like her, like, *like* like her. When we were upstairs a bit ago, I swear we almost kissed when she leaned in toward me."

He shrugs. "What's the big deal? I mean, if you can fake date, why can't you real date?"

"No, we're neighbors. It'd mess up everything. And honestly, I'm not looking for a girlfriend." I give him a pointed look. He knows about my ex and how this last year has been tough for me.

He nods and frowns. He's silent for a long beat as though thinking that statement through. "I see your point," he mumbles. "OK, so keep it professional. Draw some boundaries. Like you'll only hug or cheek kiss in front of Pierce, and otherwise, no touching."

I consider what he's saying. I mean, it's not that different from what Roxy and I have already discussed. But it's not that easy. I haven't been attracted to someone in a long time. Even with Lydia in the last year of our relationship, I can't say I was still attracted to her. I spent nearly eleven of those twelve months completely checked out from anything between us. A twinge of guilt seeps into my veins. While what she did was unforgivable, I'm not blameless in the demise of our relationship.

There's a knock at the door and we both freeze and then look at each other.

Bray walks over and opens the door.

It's Hutch.

"Well, well, well, if it isn't Bray and Gray. What's up, gentlemen?" he asks as he walks in and sits on the sofa.

"Uh, not much. What's up?" Bray asks. I can tell he's already annoyed because he hates that our nicknames rhyme, and if it was anyone other than Hutch, he'd probably point that out. Hutch is just too nice to yell at about trivial things.

"Who's up for a stakeout?" he asks.

"What?" Bray replies looking from him to me.

"Hutch, who cares about the flowers? Let's just let it stay a mystery, man," I state.

"I need to know," he says, looking defeated.

"Why?" Bray and I say in unison.

"Don't you guys ever just want answers?" Hutch asks and I feel like his question is so much deeper than just about flowers. I know Hutch is still messed up from the accident that ended his football career. He never talks about it. He's always putting on a brave face and being kind and funny, but every once in a while, I see through his façade, and I just know he's thinking about it.

"Nope," Brayden says.

"I mean, not really. Isn't it sort of fun just to have it as a mystery?" I ask.

Hutch shrugs and then glances over at me. "Why are you up here?"

Brayden gives me a look as if to ask if Hutch is allowed to know. Screw it. Everyone is likely to know eventually anyhow. Sighing, I nod.

"Gray's fake dating Roxy," he says to Hutch.

Hutch's eyes widen. "Wait, what? Why fake dating?"

I lean back again with my head staring up at the ceiling and tell him the entire story. When I finish, I put my head down and rest my elbows on my knees as I look at him.

"I mean. Roxy is hot. If you aren't serious with her, I'd ask her out," he says.

I glare at him. I just told this man that I'm attracted to my fake girlfriend. And I sure as fuck am not letting another guy date her while I have feelings for her. "Don't even try it."

Hutch grins. "I knew you liked her. It's not just about being attracted to her. There's definitely something going on between you two and it's not fake."

"That's what I was saying," Bray chimes in with a laugh. "You'd have to be blind not to notice the sexual tension between you two."

I groan and put my head in my hands. "Guys, I need real advice here."

Bray leans forward and looks at me. "Ask her out for real."

Sighing, I look at him. "I can't do that. We already have an agreement, and it would be weird."

"It's weird anyways. Who cares?" Hutch says with a laugh.

I point to both of them. "You cannot tell anyone about this."

Hutch holds up his hands in defense. "OK. No worries. I'm not saying anything. But hear me out, if she didn't like you, she wouldn't be agreeing to all of this. If there wasn't something there, she'd have walked out of that bar and left your pitiful ass standing all alone. But she didn't. So that's something."

"Fuck, Hutch. When did you get all romance-y Yoda on us?" Bray asks.

"I had lady skills back in the day," Hutch says with a smirk.

I look from one friend to the other. Maybe they are right. Maybe I should just ask her out for real? But how do I even do that? She'd probably just laugh in my face. And then, there's my worry of getting hurt again.

"Stop thinking about Lydia. She was a—" Bray starts.

I hold up a hand. "We don't need to Lydia bash tonight."

"Bray's not wrong, Gray. That woman fucked you up good. But she was all wrong for you. Roxy is...different. And maybe that's just what you need," Hutch says.

I consider his words for a long moment. He's got a point about Roxy being different. I've never met anyone like her. If anything, she sort of freaks me out. She also annoys the fuck out of me. Maybe this is a bad idea, and I should just keep it fake.

"It's not a bad idea," Bray says.

Shit, did I say that last part out loud?

Bray rolls his eyes. "I know what you are thinking. I get it. She's your neighbor. You guys got off to a rough start. This could be a big mess. But, Gray, sometimes life is messy. You need to get back on the horse, my friend."

"Plus, she reads romance," Hutch says.

"What?" I ask as my brows furrow.

"She lent me her favorite book at happy hour, and I couldn't put that fucker down. Like a great plot, but holy sex in a book. Anyhow, you should read it. I'll lend it to you, as research. I wasn't a romance fan before, but after reading that, I think I am now. And you might get some tips from it," Hutch explains.

"Down, boy," Bray teases.

"What? I'll lend it to you too. You could use some pointers. Consider it an educational fiction read," Hutch counters.

"For the love of...guys, can we focus here? I don't need a book. I just need to figure out what to do about Roxy," I say.

"Well, when are you seeing her next?" Bray asks.

"Tuesday." I look from Bray to Hutch and I can already tell I should have just gone to Al for advice.

"Bring flowers," Hutch says.

"No," I state emphatically.

"Get her talking," Bray suggests. "The more intel you get, the easier it will be to figure out how to get her to really like you."

I glare at him. "Thanks," I say, my voice laced with sarcasm.

"I just mean, you'll be able to formulate a better plan if you know her beyond her name and place of residence," he explains.

"I guess so," I mutter as I stand up. "OK, that's enough input for tonight."

"Did Kasen text either of you back yet?" Hutch asks.

We both shake our heads.

"It's not like him," Hutch mumbles as he also stands.

"I'm sure he's fine. Especially if he let Al know he was going to be away longer," I say as I open Bray's door.

"I still think we should do a stakeout at the bench," he adds as he walks behind me.

"Hutch, man, let it go," Bray says as we close the door and walk back downstairs.

We're both silent until Hutch opens his door. He turns to me, his hand still on the doorknob. "I think she'd be good for you. For the record," he says, and without another word, he steps inside his apartment and shuts the door, leaving me standing in front of mine and wondering if that is in fact true. Would Roxy Benedict be good for me?

CHAPTER THIRTEEN

Roxy

The signs are up, the inventory is audited, and I'm mentally prepping for a soft opening with family and friends in just a few days. After my near kiss with Gray, I just want to bury myself in work. I need a happily ever after and I don't think Gray would want that, or at least I assume he doesn't.

"What are you frowning about?" Jocelyn asks as she makes little party favor bags for our guests. After the whole dress thing, I had to tell her about Grayson. I'm playing it coy on our social media because the last thing I need is family and my new neighbors asking about it. Gray and I will need to talk about what to say to everyone in the building. But we'll cross that bridge later.

"I think we almost kissed last night," I blurt out and then slap my hand over my mouth. Shit, why did I have to TMI that?

Her eyebrows shoot up. "With Grayson?"

I nod, letting my hand fall to my side.

"Wow. I thought you said this was just a fake thing," she muses as she looks over at me while still folding bookstore T-shirts.

"It is," I assure her, but she gives me a pointed look and I roll my eyes. "I mean, we're meeting Tuesday to discuss it."

"The almost kiss?"

"No! The whole fake-dating thing," I correct her with an air of exasperation.

"Alright, chill. I was just asking. So, what are you going to wear?"

I roll my eyes. "Clothes, Jocelyn, clothes."

"Oh come on, you should wear—" She's interrupted by a knock at the door. I look over where we've taken down the brown paper on the window and find Carly standing there waving and smiling.

Jocelyn walks over and unlocks the door.

"Hey, sorry, I just saw your window was uncovered and I know you're having your soft opening in like a week right?" she asks.

I nod. "Yep. Everyone in the building will get invites later this week. It'll just be friends and family and a few bloggers, authors, and readers that I know well."

"Fun. I can't wait." She pauses and I know she's not here about the soft opening because she's nervously shifting her weight from one foot to the other.

"What's up?" I prod.

"You mentioned you wanted to date, and I was wondering if you had found anyone yet," she says.

"Oh, uh, sort of, why?" I ask.

"Oh, never mind, then. I was going to try to really sell you on the guys in the building," she laughs.

Jocelyn leans on the desk and crosses her arms. "Which guys?"

Carly's gaze looks toward her. "Are you looking to date?"

She shrugs. "Maybe."

"Is there more to add from our last discussion about the guys in the building?" I ask, curious what she'll say. A little more intel never hurt, right? And we've already talked about this, so I'm interested in what more she has to share.

Jocelyn shoots me a raised eyebrow and I glare at her, willing her to keep quiet.

"Well, there's Hutch. Like I said before, he's a cinnamon roll for sure. He's just a sweetie. He's silly and fun. But he has a serious side to him too. And obviously, he's adorable. Then there's Kasen. Honestly, Kasen is a bit of a mystery. I feel like I know him, but not really, if you know what I mean?"

"What's his deal anyway? Like, why is everyone worried about who checks on the sea anemones?" I ask.

"The what?" Jocelyn asks. I realize I haven't filled her in on this interesting tidbit.

"Oh, he loves sea creatures. He's a master diver. He was in the Navy, special ops. And then when he got injured, they honorably discharged him. He's totally fine, just not fit for full service anymore. He works for a contractor that sets up security software for various other government contractors and sometimes governments. He's, like, really smart. I think everyone is worried because his cousin, Elliott, always checks on things. And he hasn't replied to our texts this week. Honestly, I'm not that concerned yet, but if he doesn't reply by next week, I will be," she explains.

"Oh, OK. He sounds interesting," I state.

"He is. You'll see when you meet him. Grayson, who you know," she says as she gives me a look that either is curious or knowing, but I'm not about to test which one.

"Sort of," I say with a shrug because I want her opinion.

"Well, he's a brilliant musician as you heard at happy hour. He's very smart, like genius smart. His family is super rich, but he left the family business to pursue a music career. I think that didn't go over very well. He had a girlfriend when he first moved here, but they broke up. Otherwise, he's just a good guy. He might come off as a little…"

"Aggressive?" I ask.

"Irritating?" Jocelyn suggests.

Carly giggles. "Strong-minded," she settles on.

"What about Brayden?" I question. I see her face flush a little.

"Yeah, he's great. He's a doctor. He's been working a lot of night shifts at the ER, which is awesome for when I need help with Ava if I can't get home after school. He's friendly and kind," she says.

"So, fuck, marry, kiss," Jocelyn states deadpan.

I nudge her arm. "Jocelyn!"

"What? It's the greatest game. So?" she asks Carly.

Carly's upper body shakes with laughter. "OMG! One time Cam and I played that game in the jacuzzi. I think I said…hmmm… Fuck Hutch because…I mean former athlete, so…the muscles." She pauses and laughs. "This is so ridiculous because most of them are like brothers to me now, so ewww! But uh, kiss Kasen because he has that whole mysterious thing going on. And marry either Grayson or Brayden because they seem to have their shit together for the most part, especially Brayden."

She looks over at me and so does Jocelyn.

"What? I don't even know Kasen yet. I'm not sure I can play appropriately," I say quickly as I feel a blush creep up my face.

"So, just play along with who you know," Jocelyn counters, crossing her arms.

"What about you?" I ask her. She'd met most of my neighbors between going to the coffee shop across the street and people coming and going from the door to the building next to the shop door.

"Marry Hutch, I love me some cinnamon roll. Fuck Kasen, because he sounds like a wild time. And kiss Brayden, because he seems nice," she says, giving me a look like this should be easy.

Sighing, I lean back against a bookshelf. This isn't exactly going as planned. It's cute that Carly wants so badly to set me up with one of our neighbors, but I was hoping she would give me more insights on Gray. But now I just have more questions. "OK, fine. Fuck Hutch for the same reasons. I mean, he'd be a giver, right?" They both laugh. "Kiss Brayden because he's got some great lips. And marry Grayson because he might actually be a decent human and I don't know Kasen, so at least that's like a known option."

"See, easy," Jocelyn states but then her mouth falls open. I follow her gaze and find Gray standing at the door. It's then that the stupid bell on the door decides to work.

"Hey, I uh, was going to get coffee and decided to see if you wanted any," he offers.

Fuck me! Did he hear that? Please God do not have let him! He needs to not have heard that!

"Oh, uh, yeah, sure. I'll take a small latte with vanilla syrup," I say.

"Vanilla, huh?" he asks with a smirk. God damn it. He totally heard that.

"Yep," I state as I press my lips together.

"A mocha latte for me," Jocelyn says.

He turns to Carly. "I'm good. If I drink any more coffee, I'll be up all night. I've had like four cups already."

"Damn, lay off the caffeine, Maxwell," Gray teases her.

"I'll try, but until Ava is capable of cooking her own meals, I sort of have to be wired for my evenings," she says with a shrug.

"Valid. OK, I'll be right back," he says, closing the door and walking across the street.

The latches close and Carly starts laughing. "Fuck. I think he heard that," she says.

I bury my head in my hands as my face and neck heat with embarrassment. "That is mortifying."

"Oh, come on. It's fine. Gray is cool. I'm sure he'll just tease you about it at some point," she offers. "I mean, you all seemed cozy at happy hour the other night."

I wave her off with my hand. "No. I think we just have a truce over the shop's noise. Which is great and all. Gray and I are just...very different," I try to explain.

Carly shrugs. "Opposites attract sometimes."

"I guess. Anyhow, I hope you'll be able to come to the soft opening." I change the subject because I think I just reached my quota for embarrassment for the day.

"Wouldn't miss it!" She looks down at her watch. "OK, off to get Ava. See you all later."

"Bye," we say in unison.

"What's her deal? She's not married?" Jocelyn asks, nodding toward Carly who is walking down the street.

"No. I think she's divorced. She mentioned she's a middle school teacher the other day, but I don't know much else about her yet. She seems super sweet though," I say as I go back to my task.

Another knock at the door draws my eyes up to meet Gray's intense stare.

"I got it," Jocelyn says, opening the door.

"Latte and a mocha," he says as he reaches into the drink tray and pulls out each coffee, setting them down.

"Thanks," I reply as I take the latte.

"Sooo, how are things?" he asks, sipping his drink and looking around the store.

"Good. The soft opening is a week from Monday if you'd like to attend," I say as Jocelyn mumbles a "thank you" and then makes herself scarce.

"Of course," he says. I swear he's smirking at me.

"What?" I ask. I know my cheeks are pinker than normal and I hate my stupid pale-ass skin right now.

"Nothing. I should get going. I have some music to practice," he says as he starts toward the door.

"Oh?"

"Yeah, I'm filling in for a friend as a guest spot in the local orchestra. Should be fun. I haven't done that for a bit," he explains.

"Wow. That's cool. Let me know when. I'd love to see you play," I reply, because that's the neighborly thing to do, or at least that's what I'm telling myself.

He opens the door and pauses, looking back at me with a wide smirk on his face. "Marry, huh?"

"Oh, God. You heard that?" I say as my face goes from warm to fire-hot.

"I'll let Bray know he has great lips. He'll love that. And Hutch is a giver, is he?" he teases. I don't want to admit his lips are also kissable. I'm staring at them right now and I quickly look away because I know he saw me do it.

When I look back, I glare at him. "It was just a dumb game," I explain.

"Was it now?" He pauses and keeps the smirk on his face, and it makes my blood boil. Damn, this man can really get under my skin.

"Yes," I mutter, my jaw clenching.

"Oh, uh, Pierce is having a dinner party on Tuesday." He pauses and looks toward the back of the store where Jocelyn is pretending to be busy. "Is that OK?"

"Oh, uh, OK," I stammer.

"Just wanted to give you a heads-up since that wasn't in the plans," he explains.

I nod. "That's fine. We can talk on the way there or whatever."

"Great. I'll pick you up at five. See you later, wifey," he adds as he gives me a wink and walks out of my store.

"Wifey!" Jocelyn squeals.

"Chill, Joc. He's being a prick. Anyhow, who cares? Things can't get any more embarrassing around him, right?"

"I guess not. Thank God you didn't say fuck him because that would be hella funnier," she says as she goes back to folding things.

"Right, yeah," I mumble under my breath. Why does my fake boyfriend have to be so hot? And why does he have a knack for getting under my skin? I don't really want to answer either of those questions, I decide as I get back to work, trying my best to *not* think about Grayson Porter and his kissable lips.

CHAPTER FOURTEEN

Grayson

I stand outside the Happily Ever Afters Romance Bookstore. I can see inside now. As much as I hate admitting all that noise was for a good cause, I do see the fruits of Roxy's labor. The store is well done. I dare say I might be proud of this woman. To accomplish something this big before you're even thirty is, well, fucking impressive. I'm just turning thirty in a few months and I'm still hoping that this big break catapults my music-composing career. Fuck, I'd love to rub that in my parents' faces.

My thoughts are interrupted as I see movement in the store. I turn my head slowly and I feel the breath leave my body.

Roxy is wearing a wrap dress, and it dips low in front at the bottom of the "v" which shows off her perfect breasts, or at least what I think are perfect from what I'm seeing. Damn it. I need to stop ogling her. Fake. Girlfriend. I remind myself.

She pushes open the door and smiles at me. "Your fake girlfriend is ready."

"You look lovely," I say politely as I hold out an elbow for her. I see her stare at my arm for a long moment. She bites her lip as if she's unsure if she should touch me. I move my elbow a bit. "Your chariot awaits," I add, motioning to my car that's parked just a few buildings past ours.

"Oh, right," she answers as she cautiously loops her arm in mine. We walk silently down a half block, and I unlock the car with my fob and open the passenger door for her.

"Wow. Such service for not being a real boyfriend," she says.

I put a hand on my chest. "I've been demoted! I thought we were married."

She blushes and I fight a smirk because I love teasing her.

"Shush. We're going to forget you ever heard that, starting right now," she says as she places her long legs inside my car.

"I'll try," I say with a grin, shutting her door and walking around to the driver's side.

I slide into my seat and pull out onto Hearts Lane. I put on some classical music.

"How far is it?" she asks.

I glance over and see her hands fidgeting with the strap of a small purse. She's nervous. That surprises me a little. Roxy is an outgoing woman. I would have expected this to be an easy thing, dinner with some people, but maybe I've misjudged her.

"So..." I trail off as I choose my words carefully. "I may have told some people about our...agreement."

Her whole head swivels when she looks at me. "You what? Who?"

I glance her way. "Hutch and Bray know."

"Jocelyn knows too," she says on a sigh.

"OK, so do we tell anyone else? Because those two won't talk unless I tell them otherwise."

Shrugging, she stares at me for a long moment. "Let's just get through this dinner and we can decide after that."

"Fair enough. We need to go over some basics," I start.

"OK, like where and when we met?" she suggests.

Nodding, I contemplate the answer. "Let's say we met when you started leasing the property. We can keep it simple and like how we actually met and just bump it back a few months," I suggest.

"Oh, so when you came pounding on my door saying I was noisy?" she asks. I steal another glance and find her smirking.

"Yep. Just like that," I manage as I fight a smile. Damn, she's sassy.

"OK, so we met three months ago, the same way we actually met. When did you ask me out or did I ask you out?" she asks.

"I asked you out," I state.

She crosses her arms, which only makes my eyes focus on her pert breasts.

"Eyes up here, *hubby*," she says with a sarcasm-laced voice.

I chuckle. "I can't help it. That dress is...anyhow, let's just keep it similar to what happened."

"You mean we went on a blind date?" she asks with a raised eyebrow.

"Let's say we each confided crushes with Al and he set us up and we hit it off," I suggest.

"Or I could have asked you out?" she offers.

"Let's stick with the real story, Roxy," I growl.

Sighing again, she pushes some hair away from her cheek. "Fine," she mutters. "What else do I need to know about you?"

I feel my heart pick up speed. Shit. How much do I tell her?

"Well, uh, my parents own an investment firm and live just outside of the city. I have a younger sister, Adriana. She works with my parents, doing communications for the company. I double majored in finance and music studies at Princeton. Worked for my parents' company for a few years, and then decided to pursue music full-time. I felt like working in finance was slowly killing me. I hated everything about it and I hated working for my parents. I currently play as a guest musician in the local orchestra. I do some recording stuff with a friend who has a recording studio near our building. And I've been trying to break into film..." I pause and look at her. "I want to be like John Williams."

She smiles. "Good aspiration. What about your dating life?"

I swallow. Keep it short, Gray. "I had a long-term high school girlfriend, another in college, and a third later. I broke up with her a little less than a year ago."

"Oh, how come?" she asks.

I feel my jaw clenching. "Difference of opinions on life."

"Wow. Sounds intense," she says as she curls a leg beneath her.

"It was. What about you?" I ask, trying to take her attention away from my past love life.

"Well, I have dated a bunch of guys, but only got super serious with one of them," she admits with a shrug. I want to ask questions, but she continues. "You know about my three siblings. They are all a bunch of overachievers. My parents are just normal high-achieving parents. They live in the 'burbs. I went to college locally and studied literature. And then tried to have one serious boyfriend who I lived with for a bit and that backfired almost immediately. I ended back up at my parents' house and then my grandmother died, left me money, and I decided to try opening my bookstore. That's about it."

"I'm sorry. Were you close with your grandmother?" I ask.

She nods and looks away from me. "Yeah."

"So you lived with a boyfriend," I state.

She laughs bitterly. "Rich was a dick. I mean, the sex was great. He said I should move in way too early in our relationship. I was an idiot and said yes. It lasted a whopping four weeks before I found out he was already cheating on me." I feel my jaw clench again. "Anyhow, I packed up my things and moved home."

"Wow, sounds like an asshole," I manage through gritted teeth.

"If it talks like one and walks like one," she sighs.

"What else should I know?" I ask as I pull up to a wealthy part of the city with giant homes.

"Oh, uh...my name," she says in a low voice.

"I'm sorry, what about it?"

"It's Roxbury," she whispers.

"I'm sorry, what?"

"Roxbury!" she says loudly.

I frown trying to make sense of the name.

She turns back to me and rolls her eyes. And I know there's a story.

"I was...conceived at my parents' old house on Roxbury Street. My full name is Roxbury Anne Benedict," she mutters.

I laugh. "Wow. Well, good to know. Anything else I should know?"

"I like yoga, cats, obviously books, music, and going to planetariums," she says in rapid fire. "You?"

"Uh, I like books, mostly fantasy and spy novels, obviously music, and I've never had a pet," I say.

"What? Like never, never?"

"Yep. Never," I reply. We drive a few blocks in silence as I feel her glance at me every few seconds as if she's trying to see inside my brain.

"We're here," I announce as I pull over and park on the street. I turn to look at her. "What?"

"I'm still processing that you've never had a pet," she admits as she opens the car door and gets out.

I shake my head as I follow her up the path to a well-kept mansion. It's a stately English Tudor-style home. I take Roxy's hand in mine as we reach the front porch.

"Thank you," I whisper.

She nods as she presses the doorbell.

A minute later an older woman answers the door. "Mr. Porter?"

I nod.

"Right this way. Mr. Pointer is waiting."

Roxy stifles a giggle and I give her a curious look. "Porter and Pointer? And Gray and Bray? What's up with that?"

I chuckle and shrug. But before I can think of a response, the woman leads us into a two-story room with a fireplace and large oversized leather furniture. Pierce and Haven both stand from where they are seated and walk over to greet us.

"Lovely to see you, Roxy," Pierce says as he leans and kisses her cheek.

She blushes. "Nice to see you too."

"Grayson's been telling me all about your bookstore. I need to hear more," Haven says excitedly as she pulls Roxy into a hug and then loops her arm through hers and escorts her to a sofa.

"Well, uh, that's a conversation that could take a while, you want to get a drink, while our ladies chat?" Pierce asks.

"I'd love that," I say as I glance over at Roxy. She gives me a reassuring look and I mouth, "Thank you," again. She nods and smiles at me.

———

Dinner went surprisingly well. Apparently, the film's director, Hubert Cushner, wasn't able to attend, but it was almost better that way. I got a chance to talk with Pierce one-on-one and he assured me that the music I had written was perfect. Roxy and Haven hit it off and spent the entire night discussing books. Haven even joined Roxy's book club.

We get in the car after dinner, and I glance at the time. An idea had popped into my head around nine and I couldn't shake it, so I made up an excuse for us to leave.

"Why the rush to leave?" Roxy asks with curiosity as I pull out onto the street.

"I want to take you somewhere," I say to her. "And we need to get there before ten."

She raises an eyebrow. "Why?"

"Trust me...please," I say as I glance over at her.

She shrugs and sits back in the seat. "OK."

"OK? Like you aren't going to fight me on it?"

She glares at me. "Don't push it, Porter."

Chuckling, I turn on the music and drive us downtown. I park in the garage next door to a theater. It's a smaller, historical theater, but it has something I know she'll love. Well, a few things, I hope she'll love.

"This way," I say as I hurry us to a side door and punch in the code.

"What is this place?" she asks.

"It's the Townsend Theater," I explain. The sound of Mozart fills the air as we step through the threshold.

"What..." She trails off as I lead her up a flight of stairs to a private box. I seat her along the front and sit down next to her. Her eyes go to the stage where a quartet of strings is practicing.

My friend Yosef waves up at me as he goes to pluck a string on his double bass.

"I'll be right back," I say as I release Roxy's hand. She

glances my way but then goes back to watching my friends practice. I head to the side stage and lower the house lights and then turn on the little lights in the ceiling.

I walk back up to the box and smile as I watch Roxy staring at the ceiling in awe. I'm enjoying watching her so much, I don't move. I just stand there for long minutes as her eyes track the glittering constellations overhead and her foot taps to the beat of the music. Her hair sways gently and her lips are parted. She looks stunning, a true natural beauty. How is it possible this woman thinks she's a failure compared to her siblings? She's perfect and smart and a fucking badass business owner.

Shaking my head, I finally step up next to her and sit.

"How have I never been here before? This is beautiful," she whispers as she looks up at the ceiling.

"I agree. Beautiful," I repeat only I don't mean the ceiling. I mean Roxy.

CHAPTER FIFTEEN

Roxy

"Thank you," I say as we approach the apartment building. "That was...well, thank you."

He gives me a small smile. "I'm glad you liked it. I thought you might."

He pauses and then starts to open his mouth to say something when there's a small noise from some bushes nearby. We both stop walking.

"Did you hear that?" I ask.

He nods as he looks around. "It's probably a rat."

I roll my eyes. "Rats don't meow."

"It wasn't really a meow, was it?" he asks, but as soon as the words finish leaving his mouth, there's a sound that is most definitely a meow.

I walk over to the bushes along the front of another apartment building two buildings down from ours. I crouch down and use my phone to peer into the boxwood hedges. Two bright green eyes stare up at me.

"Well, hi there," I say softly. "Aren't you cute."

"What is it?" Gray asks as he approaches me.

"It's a dragon. What do you think it is?" I look up at him. "A rat?" I ask as I reach into the bush and extract a small black, fluffy kitten.

"I mean, it could be a rat," he says with a laugh.

"We're not a rat, are we?" I coo as I hold the kitten against my chest and stroke his dark fur. He begins to purr, his whole body vibrating with the noise.

"What should we do?" I ask, looking around as if someone will magically appear and say, "He's mine."

"I don't know," Gray says.

"Wait. You should keep..." I lift the kitten and hold it up to the streetlight. "Her."

"What? No way. I don't know a thing about cats," he says, his eyes widening as he steps away slowly as if I'm holding a small bomb.

I hold the kitten out to him. "Here, just hold her. She's very cute."

"Yeah. Well, lion cubs are cute too, but I'm not about to hold one," he protests as he continues to step back until he reaches the curb.

"Oh my God. Don't be such a pansy. Just hold her," I say as I thrust the kitten into his hands.

"Like this," I urge as I show him how to hold it against his chest. The kitten curls up and returns to purring.

"See. She likes you."

He gives me a pointed look. "She likes warmth and I'm sure food. I mean...how old is this thing? We don't have anything a kitten needs."

I pull out my phone and check the time. "There's a twenty-four-hour pharmacy not far from here. It'll have a few things. That should be enough at least until tomorrow. It doesn't look that young. We can probably feed it kitten food."

Gray sighs. "I can't really keep a cat. They're loud."

"You and noises. Come on, let's go," I urge as I take his free hand in mine and drag him back toward his car. We get in and he hands me the kitten. It buries itself against me as Gray drives us to the pharmacy where I run in and get some essentials. When I come back, I find Gray laughing. I peer inside and see he has the kitten lying on his lap. She's on her back, and every time he pokes her little belly, she holds out all her feet.

"Well, well, well, if it isn't a man and his new kitten," I tease as I open the door.

His eyes go wide. "What the heck did you buy in there?"

I put the items in the back seat. "Well, they had a litter box, not a great one, but it'll do for now. Some litter, kitten food, small metal food bowls, some toys. Just the basic cat starter kit."

"I'm not keeping it," he groans.

I sit down and look over at him. The kitten rubs its head against his hand and purrs loudly. "I think you are."

"I'm not," he grumbles, while keeping the cat on his lap as he drives us back to the apartment building.

"How come you don't park in the parking garage?" I ask as I realize he's parking on the street again.

"Hutch always backs into my car. He's replaced my bumper like three times. My car fares better out here in the wild."

I giggle. "OK, valid."

"I do park in there when it snows."

"Uh, you want me to help you bring this up?" I ask as I point to the stuff in the back of the car.

Sighing, he looks over at me and then back down at the kitten. "I really can't," he states.

"Do you need to record anything tomorrow?" I ask.

"No."

"Great. Then you can keep her tonight."

He glares at me as we get out of the car, but he keeps the kitten snuggled up against him. I grab the items I purchased and then we walk up to his apartment. I haven't actually been inside it yet and I stand at the door after he unlocks it, unsure if I should come in or just hand him the things.

He stops once he's five steps into his hallway. "You coming?"

I swallow before answering because my mouth suddenly feels dry. Why am I so nervous? Shaking my head at my strange reaction, I step inside and shut the door. I follow him, glancing at the art on the walls. We enter a living room with leather furniture. His home is, well...homey.

"What's that look for?" he asks me as he watches while I inspect his things.

"It's...nice," I blurt out and then feel like an idiot.

"Nice?" he replies with a raised eyebrow. "What? Did you think I lived in a cave?"

I fight my grin but fail. "I mean, you did kind of act like an ogre."

"I did, did I?" he muses as he pets the kitten.

"Where do you want this stuff?" I ask, raising the two bags.

He purses his lips and looks around us. "Uh, the bathroom?" he suggests.

I follow him down a second hallway and into what I suppose is the guest bathroom. He shuts a door into a bedroom and then the hall door, and in the very tight quarters, we work around each other as we fill the litter box, and he pulls down some towels from a small linen closet to make a little cat bed. I put a heating pad under it. I play with the kitten for a few minutes with one of the three toys we bought. And then we watch the kitten curl up and fall fast asleep.

"Wow. That little guy was tired."

"Girl," I correct.

"Whatever. She's tired. Now what?" He looks from the kitten back to me.

"We let her sleep. We can leave some of this food out, in case she's hungry later." I sprinkle some food into a bowl. "We'll need to get her better kitten food, but this will work for tonight."

"OK," he says slowly as he quietly opens the door and we both slip back into the hallway.

"If you need me to watch her tomorrow, just bring her downstairs," I offer as I make my way back to the front door.

"I will," he replies.

I pause when I get to the door, turning, I look back at him. He's close, just a foot away. I can smell his woodsy cologne. Why does he have to be so handsome?

"What?" he asks, his voice lower than normal.

"Nothing," I squeak, feeling foolish for ogling him. This isn't real, I remind myself for what feels like the hundredth time this past week.

He clears his throat and takes another small step toward me. "I've been thinking..." He trails off.

"About?"

"Maybe, we should kiss," he says slowly.

My eyes go to his lips and then back to his eyes. "Why?" I whisper.

"Because, won't it seem weird if we never kiss around Pierce?" he asks.

Shrugging, I consider it. "I mean, I guess it depends on how much we are around him," I counter, but somewhere deep inside, I'm screaming that I think we should practice kissing.

"I just...I thought we could have a practice one in case we have to pretend. That way it's not so awkward," he explains, his eyes drifting down to my mouth as I bite my lower lip.

His hand comes up, and he places his thumb on my lower lip, pulling it free from my teeth. He keeps his hand on my jaw as his eyes search mine.

"OK," I agree because I feel like my entire body is going to burst into flames if we don't kiss, like, right now.

He steps forward, closing the distance between us. I can feel the heat of his body as he presses it against mine. Damn, Gray has muscles, like, lots of muscles.

He chuckles as his lips brush against mine. "I work out, wife," he teases and I realize I said that out loud.

"Good, I like a hubby who's in shape," I murmur as I feel his breath against my lips.

"Do you now?" he asks, his lips coasting against mine again.

"Stop teasing me, Gray, and kiss me," I demand.

The words are barely out of my mouth when his lips crush against mine. It's the perfect amount of pressure, not too hard, not too soft. He nips a little at my lower lip and a moan escapes me. I feel my cheeks pinken, but I don't stop kissing him. His tongue traces my upper lip and our kiss deepens. Our tongues tentatively meet, with slow strokes that leave me wanting more. I whimper from the sensation, and he plunges deeper into my mouth, taking control and exploring every last crevice. Shit, is this how Gray fucks? Because if it is, then sex with him would be epic.

My arms snake around his neck, pulling him closer, needing more of him. He keeps one hand on my jaw, angling my head how he wants it, and the other holds my hip. He's somehow forceful and gentle all at once.

And then, he pulls away and drops his hands. We stare at

each other for long seconds, neither of us saying a word. The only sounds are from our labored breathing.

"Well, I guess we can check practicing kissing off our list," I finally say, breaking the silence.

He laughs and then licks his lips, and I watch his tongue as it darts out of his mouth. Damn, I'd love his tongue on other parts of my body. "I suppose we can," he says after a moment.

"Good night, Gray," I say as I turn the handle and open his door.

"Good night, Roxbury," he replies. I don't look back, but I grin when he says my given name.

CHAPTER SIXTEEN

Grayson

It's the knocking that wakes me. A constant incessant knocking. And it pisses me off because I was having a super inappropriate dream about Roxy, involving a lot more than the kissing we did last night. Fuck, I could kiss that woman for hours. Her lips were so soft. It made me wonder what the rest of her would feel like, taste like.

I roll over and put my pillow over my head, trying to block the sound. I know it's not too early because my room is slightly light even with my curtains closed.

After five minutes, I give up and walk to the hallway. I open the bathroom door, and the kitten runs out like a wild cat. Her legs go in four different directions as she attempts to scurry into my living room on my hardwood floors.

"Whoa!" I call out, chasing after her, but she's a crafty one. She manages to slide right under my sofa. And when she doesn't appear again. I get down on my knees and peek into the darkness.

"What the fuck?" I say to myself when I see absolutely nothing until I shine my phone light and see two little eyes open. "Well, shit, you really blend into the darkness, don't you."

I stand and walk into my kitchen, grabbing black licorice out of a jar and chewing on a piece while I contemplate what to do. My sister once said black licorice was my only vice. Not sure I agree with her, but it definitely is one of many vices.

I'm considering moving my entire sofa when I hear a "meow" and suddenly this little cat comes waltzing into my kitchen like she owns the place.

She looks up at me and lets out a loud, "Meow!"

"Oh, now you're hungry," I grumble as I lean down to pick her up. She tries to grab the licorice out of my other hand. "I don't think so."

I stick the rest of it in my mouth and take her back to the bathroom where I fill up her food bowl. She barely waits for the food to hit the bowl before she places her entire head inside it and starts eating it like her mouth is one of those giant claw things on a construction site.

I close the door and grab a shower. I need to go practice for my upcoming guest appearance with the orchestra.

I pull out my phone to text Roxy and see if I can drop this kitten off with her until we can figure out what to do with it when I see a missed text from Pierce.

Pierce: Hey, Haven and I are going up to the lake house this weekend, do you and Roxy want to join us? I've invited my brother, Kallen, and his wife, Amber.

I walk straight down to the bookstore. This is a conversation we need to have in person because I'm betting that we will need to share a room and I'm also betting that Roxy will not like it.

I open the bathroom door, and the cat is sitting there.

"Meow!"

"Yeah, yeah. You're real fucking cute. Come on...Licorice," I say as I pick up the kitten. She curls into a ball in my hand, and I hold her against my chest while we walk downstairs.

I tap on the door to the bookstore and Jocelyn opens it.

"Awww! Is that the kitten? Roxy told me all about her. Come see your auntie Jocelyn," she says as she swipes the cat from my arms and trots off toward a bookshelf.

"Hey," Roxy calls out from the back, waving a hand to get my attention.

"Hey," I reply because I don't know how to start this conversation.

"What's up? How's the kitten?" she asks as she stands and wipes her hands on her jeans.

"Licorice? She's fine," I reply, glancing back over at Jocelyn who is holding the kitten up like the lion cub in *The Lion King*.

"Licorice?" she asks.

I rub my temple. "Yeah, I was eating black licorice, and the name sort of stuck."

She grimaces. "Black licorice. Ew! That's, like, the worst kind!"

"No, it's the best kind." I give her a hard look and she rolls her eyes.

"Whatever. I can't really watch the kitten. Our soft opening is next week and I need to work on some things," she says as she motions around the store.

"Oh, I was hoping you could kitten-sit while I go to practice," I explain as I feel my brows furrow.

"Well, no can do. Maybe Jessa or Troy can watch her?"

I nod and swallow hard because Roxy seems to be giving off "not in the mood" vibes. What the hell?

"So, Pierce just texted me. He and Haven invited us to their lake house Friday night," I start.

Roxy full-on frowns. "Friday?"

"Yep," I answer, guessing she's going to say no.

"Joc?" she yells.

"What?" Jocelyn turns toward us still swinging the kitten.

"What time does the shipment get in on Friday?"

"It's supposed to be here by ten in the morning, why?"

Roxy looks back at me. "If, and big if, I can get those books stocked and inventoried, then I suppose I could do one night. But you owe me, big-time!" she says, poking my chest with one single finger.

"I know. Thank you," I reply from behind clenched teeth because I know she's been using us as social media fodder and this isn't a one-way street. I haven't mentioned finding her store's social media but Carly pointed it out to me a few days ago. I thought it was kind of funny and didn't mind. She didn't use my name or anything. But she's acting like it's all about her doing me a favor when in reality this is more of a two-way street.

"Is that it?" she asks.

"Yes," I reply as I turn and remove the kitten from Jocelyn's hands as I make my way to the door.

"Hey! I was playing with her," Jocelyn whines.

"Talk to your boss. She doesn't want to kitten-sit," I grumble as I hold Licorice against my chest and feel her begin to purr.

"Roxy! Come on! A bookstore cat is like...a requirement or something. She's so cute, please!" Jocelyn argues.

"No. Not now. Maybe later. We have too many packages arriving. I don't want her running out of here," Roxy barks back.

"Fine," Jocelyn says with a pout on her face. Then she turns to the kitten and smiles. "Bye, Licorice. You're such a cutie!"

Now it's me rolling my eyes as I walk outside and back

into the building, hoping Jessa will agree to babysit or maybe I can get Margie and Cornelia to do it.

———

"Uh, there's a cat back here," Roxy states as she opens my car door to put her bag inside.

"Yep. Licorice is coming with us."

"Uh, do you think that's a good idea?"

I run a hand over my face. This whole weekend might not be a good idea. "I mentioned to Pierce about the cat and Haven happened to be there and demanded we bring the kitten. Apparently, she's a huge animal lover and volunteers at some rescue. I guess they foster kittens and puppies all the time."

"Oh. OK, then. Just seems like that's a disaster waiting to happen, but it's your night," she says as she shuts the door and sits down in the passenger seat. She glances over at me as I pull out onto the street. "How long is the drive?"

"Not far. Like an hour," I explain.

"And...wait a minute," she says as if she just realized something. "How are we going to...I mean, we'll have to share a room, won't we?"

"That's the plan. But don't worry. I'll sleep on the floor," I explain.

"Great, just great," she mumbles as she crosses her arms and stares out the window.

I place a single hand on her thigh, and she glances over at me. "Everything OK? You seem...not happy."

She lets out a long sigh. "It's just..." She pauses. "Never mind."

I give her a pointed look.

"What do you care? I'm just your fake girlfriend," she says and looks back out the window.

I squeeze her thigh. "Hey," I say, softening my voice. She doesn't turn toward me, but I feel her muscles unclench a little. "I'm sorry. I'm sure this is a horrible weekend to be away, I mean with the store soft opening next week. I promise we'll leave right after breakfast tomorrow."

I let my thumb rub little circles on the side of her thigh. I don't know why I'm doing that. It just seems like the natural thing to do.

"I..." She starts but then I see her eyes looking at my hand and I stop moving my thumb and slowly pull it away. "I'm sorry. I'm just stressed out. But honestly, Jocelyn was right, it's probably a good thing to get away for a night and think about anything but the bookstore."

"Good. We can definitely distract you," I offer with a small smile in her direction.

"Meow!"

We both turn and laugh when Licorice's face is right behind us in her cat carrier, staring at us as if she's part of the conversation.

"I suppose you all will be a distraction," she muses as she looks from the kitten to me. Then she sighs and looks down at her lap where her hands are now resting. "You don't have to sleep on the floor. I'm sure they'll have a monstrous bed. We'll just put pillows down the middle or something."

"Such a romantic wifey," I tease. I see her lips twitch.

"You know me, snookums, sooo romantic," she coos in a fake voice.

"Seriously?" I ask her as I steal a glance and see her smirking. Smirking I can handle. Upset Roxy, not so much.

"What? I'm supposed to be the romantic girlfriend, right?"

I run a hand over my face. "This is going to be a big disaster, isn't it?" I ask.

"Probably, but just remember...you brought it upon your-self," she says with another smirk as she pokes my bicep.

She's not wrong about that, but right now, the thought of sleeping in a bed with Roxy is not making me regret anything, in fact, I sort of want to get to the lake house faster.

Maybe we can be fake dating with benefits? No, no. I need to stop that. I'm starting to like Roxy and that's not a good thing for her or me. With a new resolve, I turn onto the highway and hope that I can figure out a way to stop wanting to touch my fake girlfriend.

CHAPTER SEVENTEEN

Roxy

"I thought you said this was a lake house," I state as Gray pulls onto the brick-paved circular drive in front of what is a monstrous home. You can see the lake beyond the house and what looks like a small building down by a pier.

"It is," he assures me as he parks our car behind a BMW which is parked behind a Porche. Now, don't get me wrong, I've met my share of wealthy humans, I just don't normally mingle at their homes. I suddenly feel very self-conscious. Did I pack appropriate clothes? Will there be a butler serving dinner? Why was I not this nervous at their other house? I'm already stressed and anxious about Monday's soft opening. Plus, I'm confused about what is happening between Gray and me. The last thing I need is to feel like an inadequate idiot.

"Come on, Roxy. It's just Pierce and Haven. You've already met them," he says, his voice low and calm as he places that big hand of his back on my thigh and gives it a small squeeze.

I'm wearing a dress, and the material rides up just enough that his pinky finger brushes against my skin. Fuck, that feels good.

Sighing, I open my door. I need to get laid. I glance back at my fake boyfriend and consider the option of asking him if we can be friends with benefits.

"What?" Gray asks as he pulls both our bags from the trunk and pauses while inspecting me.

With a blush, I shake my head. Nope. There's no way that would work out. I want a real happily ever after and Gray has made it clear he does not. I can't handle getting hurt again, and I know myself well enough to know that sleeping with Gray would land me solidly in the broken hearts club.

"Nothing," I mumble as I straighten my dress and walk up to the front doors, yes there are two of them, giant wooden double doors with some sort of frosted leaded-glass windows in them. I go to ring a doorbell but one of the giant seven-foot doors opens and Haven squeals as she sees me.

"Yay! I'm so glad you could make it!" she says as she pulls me in for a hug, crushing me with her very tiny body. Damn, someone does Pilates.

"Thanks for inviting us," I manage before she pulls back and then steps around me to give Gray an equally big hug.

"Hey, Haven, thanks for the invite. Your lake home is gorgeous," Gray says with a grunt as Haven hugs him.

With a warm smile, she steps aside and motions for us to come into her home. We step into a large two-story foyer. It's not as flashy as I expected. There are a few paintings and lots of dark wood trim. I can see a two-story room past the hallway with floor-to-ceiling windows looking out over the lake. What must it be like to live their life? I mean, their home was insane but this is just a weekend house and it's nearly as opulent as their main house. Plus, Haven told me they have another house in LA and apartments in New York and London.

"Your room is just up here," she says as she starts up the large L-shaped staircase. "Pierce is getting the boat ready for a sunset cruise. Once you're settled, I'll take you down to the boathouse and we can get you some drinks." She pauses as she opens a door, and I gasp. It's a huge master suite with its own balcony and hot tub with a window overlooking the lake. "I hope this is alright." She looks over at us. "Kallen and Amber are down at the boathouse bar. They can't wait to meet you."

"It's perfect. Thank you," Gray offers with a smile.

"Wonderful. I'll leave you both to get settled and you can meet me downstairs in the kitchen when you're ready," she says walking back out of the room and shutting the door.

I swallow as I look around, my eyes landing on the most enormous bed I've ever seen.

"W-what kind of bed is that?" I whisper as I step up to look at the wooden headboard with metal designs on it.

"Alaska king," Gray says as if the answer is obvious. I glance at him. He's already unpacking and shoving some things in a drawer as if nothing about the opulence of this place impresses him in the least.

"Gray?" I ask as I unzip my bag but keep my eyes on him. He looks over at me.

"Yes?"

"Uh." I pause as I look around the room. No sofa, just two chairs by a fireplace and this enormous bed.

"I'll sleep on the floor if that's the issue," he mutters and walks into the bathroom holding what I suppose is his toiletry bag. What's got him so grumpy? I'm here, aren't I? I could be finishing things at the bookstore tonight, but nope, I agreed to spend the evening with Mr. Charming. I roll my eyes.

"That's not the issue," I state. "That bed is big enough for a family of five. We can both sleep in it and have our own zip code areas."

He walks back out and places his bag on a small chest. "Then what's wrong?"

I want to tell him that I think we should have rules about touching because if we do anything more than kissing like we did the other night, then I'm a goner and my heart might as well be put in a vise and squished until nothing is left of it.

I look around again. "Do you think we can use the hot tub later?" I ask instead of telling him we shouldn't touch, ever again because I might combust.

"I don't see why not," he says with a shrug.

I nod.

I place my things in the closet which is essentially a small room.

"You ready?" Gray asks from behind me.

"Yes," I reply, but before I can turn, I feel his heat against my back and his long arm reaches out and grabs a cardigan from a hanger. Holding it out for me, I slowly place each arm into the sleeves, and he pulls it taut around me.

With his arms encasing me, he whispers against the shell of my ear. "Don't want my wifey to be cold down by the water."

I feel goose bumps dot my arms and I clear my throat, desperately trying to be unaffected.

"Right," I manage.

He steps back and I feel my body sway toward his before I catch myself. Jesus, I need to get laid. I haven't gone on any dates since my ex and I broke up. Isla keeps trying to set me up with people, but I just haven't felt like dating yet. But being around Gray is making me consider the possibility that maybe I am ready to date...just date, no serious relationships yet. My heart couldn't take being broken again so soon.

"You coming?" Gray asks.

I nod, and as I follow him out, I take a photo of the giant bed and post it to the bookstore's social media with the tagline, "single-bed trope." Good thing every who knows me thinks I'm just doing a bit for my social media, otherwise these posts would be starting to cause even more issues.

I scurry down the stairs after Gray, whose long legs take leisurely strides as we walk through the house. My breath hitches at the giant living room with its two-story stone fireplace. And then I turn to see my dream kitchen. Haven is standing there organizing a tray of food.

"Oh, hey, perfect timing. Gray, could you help me carry these down," she asks as she points to a second platter of wings and some kind of fried something.

"Sure thing," he replies as he lifts the tray in one hand and grabs the second tray as if they weigh nothing.

"I can carry one," Haven insists.

"No worries. I got them. Lead the way," Gray states as Haven opens a sliding door and Gray walks out onto a deck and then down a few stairs to the lakefront. I follow them, feeling a little useless. The temperature drops as we reach the water, but the bar along the side of the boathouse has space heaters, which helps a little.

A man and woman are sitting at the U-shaped bar and Pierce is at the grill.

"Hey, welcome," Pierce says as he puts down some tongs and comes around the bar to kiss me on the cheek and shake Gray's hand.

"Thanks for having us," I reply.

"This is my brother, Kallen, and his wife, Amber." He turns to us. "And this is Grayson Porter and Roxy Benedict. Gray's doing the score for my film."

"Nice to meet you," they answer in unison and then look

at each other and laugh. It's clear these two are very much in love.

"Roxy is opening a romance bookstore," Haven says to Amber.

Amber's eyes widen. "Really? Where? When does it open?"

I giggle and sit down next to her as Roxy takes the seat on my other side. We begin a discussion, where I have to pretend my social media story is fake. This just keeps getting more and more complicated.

"Hey, I thought you said you were bringing a kitten?" Pierce asks Gray. Gray's face turns white. I can see the blood drain from it as I watch him talk with Pierce.

"You alright?" Pierce asks.

"Fuck, Licorice," Gray blurts out and takes off running up the steps without saying another word. Fuck. How could we have forgotten the kitten? I mean, it's only been five minutes and it's not hot outside, but still. We are officially the worst pet parents. I stand to go follow him.

Kallen laughs. "Dude, he must really like licorice."

"It's a kitten," I say. "I'm guessing you knew that we were bringing her?" I add as I glance over at Pierce.

"Yeah, he asked about it. Where is she?" Pierce asks.

Sighing, I start up the steps. "She's in the car."

Before anyone else can ask, Gray appears on the deck with Licorice swaddled in a blanket. She looks perfectly content and also like she just woke up.

I walk up to meet them. "She looks fine. It was only for a few minutes."

He runs one hand over his face. "I can't believe I left her in the car."

"Well, it's not hot out and it wasn't for long," I try to assure him.

"Thank God I have no kids. I'm the worst parent ever," he chastises himself.

"It's OK," I insist reaching out to run a hand over his jaw, trying to placate him.

"No, it's not," he whispers from behind clenched teeth.

Damn, we're quite the pair today. Maybe my moodiness has rubbed off on him.

I take a deep breath. "It's new. We both need to do better. We'll do better. OK?"

I mean that in so many ways, but Gray looks down at the kitten and back at me. "OK," he finally says and we walk back down to the boathouse.

"There she is," Pierce says. "Haven loves cats. Not sure if you saw our two at home when you came over."

"I'd bring them here, but they hate the water," Haven states as she motions to the lake.

Licorice, on the other hand, is completely unbothered by anything. She's sprawled on her back in Gray's arm, her eyes barely open.

"Is it alive?" Kallen teases.

Gray strokes Licorice's belly and she purrs. "Yep. No thanks to her idiot parents, but she's fine."

"One time, we left our two-year-old at my parents' house in our haste to get our twins home for a nap. He was so quiet, playing in their family room while watching a cartoon and we were so tired because the babies weren't sleeping. Anyhow, my parents called us five minutes into our drive home. We had to turn around and go back to get him," Amber admits.

"My parents left me at a funeral once," Pierce laughs.

We all turn to him.

"My mom was upset. It was her dad's funeral. I'm one of five kids and I guess everyone thought everyone else had me," he explains with a shrug.

Haven pulls out beers and places them on the bar top. "I think we could all use these," she announces with a smile.

And just like that we all laugh and grab drinks and food and go back to talking. Amber, Haven, and I spend the entire evening discussing our latest reads.

Every so often, I catch Gray watching me, but he looks away as soon as we make eye contact. I'm not sure why, but my heart flutters a little each time we lock gazes.

———

"How are we doing this?" Gray asks as we enter our bedroom after a fun evening of eating and drinking. Licorice did wake up eventually and everyone played with her until she ate and then fell back asleep.

Gray placed her litter box in the bathroom. We both look at the bathroom and then the bed.

"We'll do a Licorice-up-the-middle formation," I announce as I grab my bag and go into the bathroom, changing into my black cat pajamas, which seemed appropriate. When I finish and come back out, Gray looks over at me and chuckles.

"So, you're saying you have a thing for black cats?" he asks.

But I can't speak because Gray is wearing light sweatpants and only that and our kitten is curled up in one of his arms against his very naked chest while he reads something on his phone. He's wearing glasses and fuck does he look sexy.

"You coming to bed?" he asks without looking up again.

"Yeah," I manage as I shut my mouth.

"Stop staring. You're going to give me a complex," he states as he swipes his phone screen.

I look away and quickly crawl onto the bed, turning out the light on my side.

As I curl on my side facing away from him, I feel a warm little body press against the back of my legs. I look down and see that Licorice is making herself at home.

"Well, I see who is her favorite," Gray grumbles as he turns out the light on his side.

"What can I say? The cat has class," I tease.

"I guess."

"Gray?"

"Yes?" he answers and I turn my head to find him facing me. I turn and place Licorice between us where she curls back into a ball.

"I had fun tonight. Let's stay and go for a boat ride tomorrow. Pierce said it'd only be for a few hours. Then we can go home," I say, surprising even myself. But it's relaxing out here and the company is good and I think Jocelyn was right about needing a night off.

"If you're alright with that," he confirms.

"I am," I say and I watch as he leans over and kisses my cheek. His five o'clock shadow brushes against my skin and damn it if my lady parts don't come to life.

"Good night, wifey," he says in a gravelly voice as he pulls back.

"Good night, husband," I reply and I lean forward and plant a kiss on his lips for reasons I'll never understand. Maybe I've wanted to all day? Maybe I'm caught up in the moment? Either way, I'm not ready to unpack any of that.

He doesn't pull away and neither do I. Our lips stay pressed together for way too long.

"Gray?" I finally whisper against his mouth.

"Yes?" I feel his hot breath caress my skin.

"It's a shame this is fake because you are a good kisser," I admit with a blush. I'm happy it's dark because he can't see my skin.

"So are you, Roxy. Any man would be lucky to have you,"

he replies as he places another small kiss on my lips while his left hand roves over my hip and side before caressing my ass.

I let out a small moan.

"We should...go to bed," he says but I can tell he wants anything but that.

"We should..." I trail off as his hand presses my ass so that my hips collide with his, our bodies creating a "v" around Licorice.

"What if..." This time he trails off.

"What?" I ask, looking into his eyes in the dim light of the room.

"What if we changed our agreement?" Holy shit. Is he wanting to make this physical? Do we both want that? Do I really want that? I mean, yes, Gray is hot as fuck, but can I handle that?

"Like what?" I inquire.

"Like...we could be more physical," he offers as his hand strokes my backside.

I lick my lips. "How much more physical?"

"You tell me when to stop," he says as he picks up the kitten and places her on a pillow on the other side of him and then he pulls me flush against his body, against his erection. Shit, am I about to see all of Gray? God, I hope so.

CHAPTER EIGHTEEN

Grayson

"Breathe, Roxy," I say in a low voice as I run my nose along hers. Damn, her body feels so good against mine. I know we shouldn't do this. It's a bad idea. It may actually be my very worst idea, but right now, all I can think about is Roxy's insanely hot body. I'll admit half the reason I put that cardigan on her was to cover up her body from anyone seeing it. That dress left little to the imagination. Fine, that's a lie. My imagination had zero trouble imagining me peeling it off her.

She lets out a breath and I press my lips to hers again. Her hands touch my chest and then move up to my hair. She scratches my scalp with her nails and fuck that feels good.

"Keep doing that," I urge as I grip her ass harder. She has the perfect ass. I need to see it. I've never needed to see an ass more than hers. I push down the waistband of her pajama bottoms until her entire ass is exposed. Then I purposefully kiss her jaw and neck and peer over her shoulder down at those fucking perfect ass cheeks. The thought of them bouncing as I fuck her from behind clouds my vision.

She places one leg over my hip and starts grinding against my cock as she moans.

"That's right, baby, make yourself come," I demand as I press myself against her hot core. My hands come around her waist and I slide a hand inside her pajama bottoms and then slip inside her panties. Her bare skin is hot and wet as I slide a single finger along her folds and then gently circle her clit. She moans again.

"Don't stop!"

I keep going, wanting to see her come undone from my touch. Her eyelids are closed and her long lashes tremble against her flushed cheeks. She's gorgeous. Far more gorgeous than any other woman I've been with.

My finger circles her engorged flesh, rubbing wetness around as my other hand grabs her breast, my thumb flicking against her nipple.

Her hips grind faster and my cock feels like it's going to burst. Her hand comes between us and I feel it slide into my sweatpants. She wraps her hand around my tip and then the top half of my cock that she's not grinding against and God damn, she feels good.

"Fuck yeah," I whisper against her jaw.

"I'm so close," she says as I feel her growing wetter, her flesh becoming more swollen. I find a rhythm with my fingers, and when she starts to tremble, I try to keep up the pace which is hard because I'm nearly coming myself with her hand stroking me.

"Right there, don't stop," she says in a breathy voice and then her body goes rigid as her lips fall open in a silent cry. Something about watching her unravel from my touch pushes me over the edge. Her strokes pick up pace as her body relaxes, and within seconds, I'm coming all over her hand.

We both pant, our hands still touching the other's body, but no longer moving. I pull my fingers away first, bringing them up to my mouth to lick them. Her eyelids flutter open and she watches me, her hand still on my cock, wet with my release.

"That's hot, Gray," she says with a smirk as she reaches behind her and grabs a tissue. Then she pulls her hand free and wipes it off but not before she brings it to her mouth where she licks it clean.

I groan. "Fucking hell, Roxy. Are you trying to one-up me?"

She giggles. "Maybe," she says, drawing out the last syllable.

I grin at her and she grins back. I'm about to suggest we take this to the next level, when all of a sudden, she looks over my shoulder, and her eyes go wide.

"Where's Licorice?" she yelps as she sits up and looks around the room.

I sit up next and pat the pillow but there's no cat.

"Damn it. Licorice!" I call out as if the damn cat is going to answer me. We both climb out of bed.

"Licorice!" Roxy says loudly as we each begin searching the room. She's on her knees looking under the bed. I walk into the bathroom but see no kitten.

"Does she know her name?" I ask myself because I literally named her days ago.

"Holy fuck!" Roxy yells and I race out to find her pushing the sliding door. I make it to the doorway and see Licorice on a tree branch that hangs by the small balcony.

"Roxy, wait," I command as I step forward and put a hand in front of her because I swear this woman is about to climb out onto this limb after a damn cat.

"I can reach her," she argues, trying to push my hand away from her abdomen.

"No," I growl as I step in front of her. I push a chair over, stand on it, and reach out toward Licorice. "Come here, sweetie," I coo.

She meows but doesn't budge aside from rubbing her little face against a small branch.

"What do we do?" I ask, beginning to feel panicked. Not only did I leave this furry bundle in the car for five minutes, I totally left the slider open and now she could fall to her death.

"Food," Roxy whispers and runs back to the bathroom. She holds out the food to me and I shake it a little. Licorice looks my way and starts to walk toward me.

"That's right," I say. I lean forward a little and she gets within arm's reach of me. I grab her but lose my footing. I lean back and turn as I start falling and then suddenly I'm crashing into Roxy and we both go tumbling onto a lounge chair. I manage to catch myself with one hand while keeping Licorice in the other.

I stare down at Roxy who has wild eyes and is searching my body.

"Oh my God! Are you OK?" she says as her hands run over my arms.

I let myself relax a little as I realize I'm not injured and the damn kitten is safely tucked between our bodies looking innocent.

"Yes," I grumble as I look down at Licorice, "no thanks to this furball."

Roxy starts to laugh and the kitten shakes between us. "Oh my God! We should not be allowed to be parents, like ever!"

I can't help the smile that forms on my face. This entire thing is ridiculous. I just got cockblocked by a kitten who almost got me killed.

"We should probably go to bed," Roxy says and then adds, "After we lock all the doors."

I chuckle as I stand and hold out a hand for her. She leans down and picks up the food bowl that spilled on my fall and then takes my hand as I pull her up to stand in front of me.

"Come on, before we all fall over the deck," I demand as I put a hand on the small of her back and guide her toward the bed. I slide the door closed and shut the closet door so it's only the bathroom and bedroom where this little furry missile can run.

Roxy climbs into bed and so do I.

"Tell me about little Grayson Porter," she says sleepily as she curls up against me. "Put our holy menace in between our pillows." She pushes the pillows apart and I set Licorice in between them. Licorice, seemingly unaffected by all her adventures today, curls into a ball and falls asleep.

"Fucking cats," I mutter.

Roxy giggles. "Now, now, we did sort of fuck up...again."

"I don't know if we should keep this cat, Roxy. So far we left her in a car and now we've left a door open," I state as I watch Licorice sleep.

"Two rookie moves. But we'll figure it out. Let's give it a few weeks," she urges. "Please." Her eyes look so hopeful that I can't say no.

"OK. Three weeks," I say.

She grins. "Don't be such a grump. We'll figure it out. I promise. I'm just out of cat practice. Now, back to little Grayson. Did you always play instruments?"

Careful with facts, I share little snippets of my childhood and how my grandmother gave me a violin when I was eight. How I loved music and would spend hours playing instruments. How nothing brought me greater joy than learning a new piece of music. Eventually, Roxy's breathing slows. Her even breaths indicate she's fast asleep. I lie there watching her for hours. Can I trust her? Can I be what she needs? I don't know.

———

"I'm glad we stayed," Roxy murmurs against my ear as Pierce steers the boat through a canal near his home. Roxy is pressed against my side on a double seat at the back of the boat. My arm is around her shoulders. I hate admitting that I love her here with me. It took all my willpower not to peel off her clothes this morning, but Licorice had made a bed between Roxy's breasts and the two of them were fast asleep when I woke, so I went for a run in Pierce's gym and showered before waking her with a gentle kiss.

She called it a *Sleeping Beauty* moment and smiled against my lips and damn it if I didn't love everything about that.

"Let it rip, Pierce! We need speed," Kallen chuckles as we start toward Pierce's house after cruising around for two hours.

Pierce starts speeding up and heads out around the corner of the channel. As we turn, a large boat appears around the corner. He slows and turns abruptly. I grab the seat cushion as the boat pitches high on one side, then another, and then higher. I go to grab Roxy but then as Pierce tries to throttle the boat to get out of the enormous wake, she grabs the side of the boat, and her hand slips. She goes flying overboard.

"Roxy!" I scream, and without any other thought, I leap in after her.

"Fuck. Man overboard!" Pierce yells and I hear the engine kick off.

I look around wildly, trying to spot Roxy. Her head pops up to the surface and I grab her, pulling her against me as I kick my legs. "I got you, baby. I got you," I whisper as I hold her trembling body. Thank God it's not too cold, but it's still chilly in the morning with the lake breeze.

"Here," Kallen says as he tosses us a life raft. We stupidly didn't have life jackets on and I'm kicking myself for yet another failure this weekend that could have ended in tragedy. What the fuck is wrong with me?

I grab the life raft and manage to get us to the little ladder on the back of the boat. Pierce is there, helping to pull us up, taking Roxy from me while Haven wraps her in a warm blanket.

"You OK?" he asks, his face laced with concern.

"Yeah, I'm good," I say but mostly I'm pissed at the boat that came out of nowhere and almost killed my fake girlfriend...my real girlfriend? I don't even know what we are now.

"Roxy, you OK?" he asks as he bends down to examine her.

"I—I'm OK," she stammers as I sit down next to her and begin rubbing her arms, trying to raise both our body temperatures.

"Let's get her back. She needs a warm shower and some dry clothes. And so do I," I say, glad we aren't far from the house.

Pierce carefully maneuvers us home. He pulls up and I help Roxy out of the boat. Her lips are a little blue as I take her in my arms even though she protests.

"I'm fine," she protests.

"Not happening. We are getting you in the shower now," I growl as I carry her up to the house with everyone in tow.

"I'll make tea," Haven offers.

"Let us know if you need anything," Pierce adds. "Sorry," he mouths. It's not his fault. The other boat was in the wrong, cutting so close to the channel at a speed higher than it should have been. And the fact they didn't even stop when we went overboard makes me rage with anger.

"She'll be fine. I'll just get us warmed up before we head home," I assure them as I give him a tight smile. I know they are concerned but not nearly as concerned as I am.

I carry Roxy straight into the bathroom and turn on the shower. I start peeling off her clothes and mine. She slaps me away.

"I got it," she mumbles.

"Let me help," I offer as I dry myself with a towel from the warming rack and start putting on warm, dry clothes.

"Gray! I. Got. It." She glares at me.

I put my hands up in defeat. "OK, OK. I'm just trying to help."

Sighing, she pulls her wet shirt over her head. I swallow hard. Her white bra might as well be translucent and damn her breasts are gorgeous. I'm definitely going to hell for thinking of them like this considering what just happened.

"Uh, I need to get out of these wet clothes," she mutters as she motions for me to leave.

"OK." I start to step back, but instead, I step forward and pull her tightly against me, pressing a kiss to her forehead. "I'm sorry," I say.

"It's not your fault. That other boat was clearly driven by an asshole," she says.

Her body relaxes a little as I rub her back.

"Get warm. I'll bring up the tea," I say as I release her and walk downstairs.

"How's our fish?" Pierce asks.

I chuckle. "She's OK. She's showering."

"Poor Roxy. Here's some tea," Haven says as she hands me a warm mug.

"Thanks. I'll take it up to her," I say as I turn and head back upstairs.

"Roxy," I start as I walk inside.

She's giggling.

"Roxy?"

"I'm in the shower," she calls out.

"What's so funny?" I ask in confusion.

"I have a shower buddy," she replies.

"You what?" I reply as I step toward the bathroom door which is cracked open.

"Uh, Licorice likes the shower," she says bursting into giggles again.

My body immediately relaxes at the happy sound. My woman is going to be OK. Shit, *my woman*? I push aside that thought.

"Well, when you two finish, I have tea," I say.

"Thanks, I'll be out in a flash," she replies, and I hear the shower turn off.

A minute later, a towel-covered Roxy opens the door. Licorice is also wrapped in a towel. I grin.

"So we have a water cat?" I ask as I peer down at the wet bundle in her arms.

"We do. I suppose it's payback for our bad parenting," she says with a giant grin.

"Here." I hand her a mug and she hands me the cat.

"Shall we go home?" I ask.

She nods. "I think we've had enough fun for one weekend, no?"

"Agreed. We can get lunch on the way," I offer.

Nodding, she sets the mug down and walks toward the closet. When the door opens, she drops the towel, leaving her naked backside facing me.

My breathing stops as I stare at her perfect ass.

She glances over her shoulder. "It would have been more fun if we were skinny-dipping," she teases as she winks at me and walks inside.

I run a hand over my face as I stare down at Licorice. "I'm screwed, aren't I?"

"Meow!"

"Yeah, that's what I thought. Let's get your troublemaking ass packed," I state as I start picking up things in the room, but my eyes continue to dart toward Roxy as she dresses, giving me peeks of her body with each move. Fuck, the drive home is going to suck because I have the worst case of blue balls that I've ever had in my life.

CHAPTER NINETEEN

Roxy

After assuring everyone that I was fine and then agreeing to stay for lunch, we finally made our way back home. Even with falling into the water, it was a fun weekend. The only glaring issue...it is beyond clear that something changed between Gray and me, and I have no idea how I feel about that.

Gray dropped me off yesterday, gave me a gentle kiss, and then left. What does that mean? Are we still faking this thing? I had so many questions but I couldn't find the right words. Am I ready to date again? I don't know. And Gray seemed against dating too. Has that changed? I know we need to talk but it seems too overwhelming with everything else going on.

I stare at the gift bags for my soft opening before picking one up to examine it. I can't believe it's on Monday.

We'll have some limited hours for the next three weeks and then we'll have a grand opening. In the meantime, our online store is going to be fully operable this week and our in-store book clubs will begin in two weeks. I wanted a phased-in approach so I could adjust things without being overwhelmed.

Placing the bag back in the pile, I decide to get myself a coffee. I walk over to the coffee shop and find Cam refilling the coffee machine.

"Hey," she says warmly.

"Hey," I reply as I lean against the counter.

"Everything OK?" she asks with a frown.

"It's fine. I..." I trail off as I watch Hutch dressed in hunting gear walk to the park.

Cam leans forward and watches him.

"What the hell is he doing?" I ask.

Cam laughs. "He's trying to scope out the flower situation."

"They're already out there," I point out as I motion to the bench.

"I know. He thinks he can, like, set up a motion camera or something. I don't know. I heard him yapping about it to Gray this morning," she says with a shrug. "Personally"—she leans in conspiratorially—"I prefer to leave it as a mystery."

"Me too. I think. Speaking of mysteries, has anyone heard from Kasen yet?" I ask.

"Not yet, but Al keeps assuring us he's fine," she says with a shrug.

"Are there always so many mysteries here?" I ask as I consider what to order.

"Just the flower one. Kasen is just...well, he's Kasen. You'll get it when you finally meet him," she says.

"Caramel latte today," I order.

She gets to making my coffee. And I turn to see Gray leaving the building. He's dressed in a suit, and damn, he looks good. The memory of his hands on my body makes a fire begin in my core.

I watch him as he approaches Margie who is walking down the street. He takes her arm, walks back to the door, and opens it for her. Fuck. He's a good guy. Damn it. Why does he have to be so good? It was easier when I didn't like him or was ambivalent in some sort of mutual-satisfaction, fake-relationship bliss, but now...well, I like the guy, a lot.

"What are you...oh," Cam says as she looks over at Gray.

I blush as I see realization dawn on her face.

"So, you like Gray," she states with a smirk and goes back to making my latte.

I bite my lip because we agreed not to share our fake relationship but we never talked about sharing crushes on each other. Not that he has a crush on me, that'd be ridiculous. Although, we did kiss and then make out. Why does this have to be so damn confusing?

"What?" Cam says, interrupting my thoughts.

I shake my head. "Nothing. Uh, yeah, I guess I do like Gray. He's a good guy."

She frowns. "OK, like you *like* like him? Or you just like him?"

I roll my eyes. "I guess I really like him."

"Hmmmm. Interesting," Cam says as she finishes making my drink.

"What's interesting about that?" I ask.

"Well, Drew said you guys weren't compatible and I said you'd make the perfect couple," she says.

I frown. "Why did he think that?"

Shrugging, she hands me my drink. "Who knows? I think it was because he pegged you as wanting a happily ever after and he knows Gray is anti-dating at the moment, so not exactly stellar relationship-match material."

"Why *does* Gray not want to date? Is it really just because of his last breakup?" I question.

She shrugs. "He was dating this woman when he moved in

and they broke up. He took it pretty hard. He thought she would stick with him while he worked on pursuing his dream. I guess that's why," Cam explains.

For the first time since I've met Grayson Porter, I really consider the fact that this man had an entire existence before I arrived in his life. I also start to think about the fact that I don't really know that much about him. Whenever we talk about pertinent things we need to know, it's always basic information or random life stories. Aside from knowing his parents live not far from here and his younger sister lives on the other side of the city, he just says he isn't close with his family and his upbringing was...what did he call it? Ah, yes, *unremarkable*.

"Did you ever meet her?" I ask because I suddenly have a million questions.

"Yeah, a few times. She came to happy hour like a couple of times but didn't seem to really gel with anyone. And then I saw her in passing once or twice and a few times they came by here to get coffee." She leans over the counter and lowers her voice. "Between you and me, if you aren't a cop, a doctor, or nurse, or someone who has to work a graveyard shift and you ask for black coffee no sugar, no cream, I'm silently judging you."

I chuckle. "Noted. Glad to hear I'm not being judged for my lattes."

"Hell no, latte orderers are the best," Cam replies with a wink.

The door opens and we both startle. I turn to find Hutch holding the door open for Jocelyn. Their size difference is almost comical. Jocelyn literally walks beneath his outstretched arm. I'm half-tempted to start calling him Tarzan.

"How's your stakeout coming along?" Cam asks with a raised eyebrow.

Hutch sighs. "If work didn't get in my way, I could commit to more surveillance. I'm hoping that I can capture the culprit with my motion sensor camera."

"Culprit? Seriously?" I state with a roll of my eyes.

"Culprit, secret flower person, whatever. I need to know," he says emphatically.

"The guardian of Hearts Lane Park," I correct because that's what the notes always say. He shrugs.

Jocelyn nods and looks up at him. "I agree. The mystery is killing me."

A moment later, the door opens again, and Carly and Brayden walk inside.

"Where's your mini me?" Cam asks Carly.

"She has a field trip today. I wanted to chaperone, but my students have this big test coming up, and I needed to help them prepare. This single parenting is for the dogs," she grumbles.

Brayden wraps his arm around her shoulders and squeezes it. "You're doing great," he assures her before dropping his arm. "Two cappuccinos," he says to Cam.

Cam laughs. "Bray, if I don't know your usual orders by now, then I'm like the worst friend in the history of friends. Large cappuccinos, sugar-free vanilla syrup, three shots of espresso, and almond milk."

Hutch gives her a hard look and she rolls her eyes. "Small dirty chai tea latte with regular milk and two shots of espresso."

Hutch grins. "And that's why I love you."

Cam's second eye roll is followed by a smile. I can't blame her. It's hard to stay mad at Hutch. He gives off giant teddy bear vibes.

"Hey, Roxy," Hutch greets me as he stands between Jocelyn and me. Carly and Brayden discuss some show they are both binging after greeting each of us. How those two aren't dating is beyond me.

I turn to look out the café's window. Gray is there and opens the door.

Our gazes meet and we stare at each other for a long several seconds. It's like the entire world around us disappears. A small part of me concocts a half dozen plausible romance novel moments that could occur right now. Gray could walk straight toward me and take my face in his hands and kiss me. He could remember that I love the double-chocolate muffins here and buy me one and then break a piece off and slowly feed it to me while looking at my mouth with need in his eyes. He could ask for extra whipped cream on a latte and then dip his fingers in it while staring at me and slowly suck the cream off them. Damn...that would be hot.

"You OK, Roxy? You look flushed," Hutch asks as his giant hand flies up to check my forehead.

"I'm good. Just got a little overheated. Must be too much caffeine," I say, the words coming out too quickly as I look away from Gray's intense stare.

Carly looks at me with a raised eyebrow and I look down as I reach into my pocket and grab my phone to pay for my coffee. Cam is also giving me a suspicious look as I press my phone to the scanner.

"OK, well, I'll see you all later. I hope you'll be at the soft opening," I say to my neighbors.

The door opens again and Drew walks inside.

"Wow, building meeting or have we just synced up all our period cravings," he teases.

Gray, Brayden, and Hutch groan, and Drew laughs. "Chillax, bros, I'm teasing. My usual, Cam," he says.

"Later," I call out again as I brush past both Gray and Drew in a hurry to get away from all the scrutiny. The more I get to know everyone, the harder it is to pretend to be in a relationship with Gray, that is *if* we are still pretending.

"Roxy!" I hear Gray's voice call out as I unlock the store's door.

I turn to see him jog across the street. I watch his hair sway and his muscles bunch with each stride. Why did he have to end up being so perfect? It was easier when I was annoyed by him. It was easier before I started falling for him. But now, I wonder if this could actually work. Do we have a real shot at a happily ever after? Maybe.

I'm contemplating that thought as Gray slows and walks the last few steps toward me.

"Inside," he growls as he pushes the door open all the way and I walk backward as he steps forward, looking more like a lion on the prowl than a man coming to talk to his pseudo-girlfriend.

I swallow hard as he corners me behind some shelves away from the window of the store. When my back hits books, he takes the coffee from my hand and sets it down before placing his hands on either side of my face.

His lips press firmly against mine and I sink against his hard frame as my arms come up around his neck, pulling him closer. Holy fuck! It's like he read my damn mind.

Our kiss turns frantic, a desperation I've never known claws at me. His tongue explores me as if he's marking me with it, claiming my mouth as only his. One hand trails down my neck and settles on my waist, his thumb slowly caressing the underside of my breast through the fabric of my shirt and bra.

But just as abruptly as he started, he pulls back. We're silent other than our ragged breathing as we both stare wildly at one another.

I lick my lips which are still wet from our kiss.

His hand that's still on my jaw moves so his thumb swipes along my lower lip. I suck it into my mouth, and he groans.

"What are you doing to me, wifey?" he murmurs, his eyes searching mine.

I swallow hard before answering. "I'm...I don't know...I'd like to ask you the same thing."

His lips twitch and then form a smirk. "We're fucked. Aren't we?"

"Probably," I agree, still breathless.

His hands drop away. "I need to go. I'll see you at your opening."

"Soft opening," I clarify.

His hand comes back up and cups my jaw, his thumb stroking affectionately over my cheek. "It'll be great." He pauses and looks around us. "I'm proud of you. You've done an amazing job here. I'll admit, I was skeptical, but I was so very wrong about you, Roxbury Benedict."

He leans forward and places a gentle kiss on my lips, barely touching them. When he pulls away, his eyes stay glued to mine.

"You're a successful businesswoman. Don't let anyone tell you differently, ever," he says sternly.

I nod because words fail me. His hand falls back to his side and he takes my coffee, holding it out for me. I pick it up and watch as he leaves the store.

Holy shit! I just lived a book boyfriend scene in real life.

CHAPTER TWENTY

Grayson

"I can't believe a freaking trash panda stole my camera!" Hutch says as he sips his drink.

"Dude, let it go." Drew interjects as he pulls a book off the shelf and reads the back. We're all at the soft opening of the bookstore.

To say I'm impressed is an understatement. Around fifty people are milling around. There are two authors signing books in the back of the store. A caterer and two staff walk around with appetizers and there's a small bar set up by the front desk that's serving beer and wine. Everyone attending has received a bag full of books and bookish items.

If this is her soft launch, I can't wait to see what she does for her official grand opening day.

"I'm going to get to the bottom of it. I just need to figure out a new plan," Hutch grumbles as he looks over at the book Drew is holding. His eyes widen and I lean down a little to see what he's looking at. A shirtless alien man who looks way more ripped than even Hutch or Kasen. I mean, Brayden, Drew, and I are fit, but even I have to admit Hutch and Kasen are next-level gym rats. Hutch might have a slight limp from his football-ending injury, but he's made up for it by being able to lift small cars or at least I would assume he can. I can never keep up with him at the gym.

"Alien why choose romance?" Cam asks as she takes the book from him.

"I didn't know that was a thing. Clearly, I need to read more," Drew quips as he looks around the shelves. "What else is in here?"

Cam takes Drew's hand. "Come on, let's go get these books signed," she says as she pulls two books out from her tote bag.

Hutch steps closer to me after they leave. "So, how are things going?" He motions to Roxy who is talking to her brother. I've been introduced to her entire family tonight. They are all very nice and normal. She introduced me as her good friend. Which was what we had planned on doing, but I admit it made me wish that she considered me her real boyfriend. I could see her younger sister, Isla, eyeing me up as if she knew something more was going on between us. I played up how impressive Roxy is because I know that she comes from a family of overachievers and doesn't think she is one as she's alluded to previously. However, it is clear she is, because only an overachiever could pull off a party like this for their soft business opening.

"Fine," I say as I drink my beer to avoid giving any more detail.

"Fine? Bro, I see the way you are staring at her. That is not how you look at a *fake* girlfriend. That's how you look at the woman you want to bear your children."

I glare at him. "We have an arrangement. That's all. Nothing more," I mutter.

"Oh, I think there's more. Maybe you just don't know it yet," he says with a smirk. "OK, I'm off to find another." He raises his empty bottle and heads in the direction of Jocelyn and the bar. I'm half-curious if he's into her, but I have my own romantic issues to deal with.

I pretend to be interested in a book, to avoid looking at Roxy. If Hutch can see through my bullshit pretending, then so can everyone else, and I don't need five hundred questions right now as I'm attempting to figure out what *is* happening between Roxy and me.

"I didn't peg you as a BDSM erotica reader." Roxy's voice interrupts my thoughts. Shit. I look down, actually reading the back cover and then grimace as I place the book back on the shelf.

"Hey, no judgment. That's a bestseller," Roxy teases.

"It's going well," I say as I try to change the subject.

She follows my gaze as we both look around the store. "It is. Thanks for being here."

I look back at her. "Of course. I wouldn't have missed it."

She glances over at her family who are all talking to one another.

"Your family seems nice," I state as I nod in their direction.

Blushing slightly, she looks back at the bookshelf. "They are," she responds but I feel like there's more to that answer.

"Your parents look proud of you," I add because it's true and I feel like she needs her self-confidence built up a little.

She rolls her eyes. "I set the bar pretty low, so I suppose anything I do above a mediocre college degree and an asshole boyfriend is pretty fucking impressive."

I want to take her hands in my face and tell her that she is one of the most impressive people I know, but I can't. Instead, I ball my hands into fists to fight the itch to touch her.

"Don't do that," I growl in a low voice.

Her eyes fly up to look at mine. "Do what?"

"Undersell yourself. Look around you. You did all of this." I put my hands on her shoulders and turn her to look at the party in the bookstore she created.

"I know," she breathes in a quiet voice. "I should...go mingle." She pulls away from me. It takes all my self-control not to go grab her by the arm and haul her ass up to my apartment and show her how impressive, beautiful, and smart I think she is.

I walk over to the bar and grab another beer. I'm about to go find Bray and Carly when I see Margie and Cornelia walk into the party. I frown wondering if they misread the invitation because they are dressed like they are going on the Titanic. Margie is wearing a literal fur shawl over a purple dress complete with a strand of pearls. She has a matching purple hat on her head. Cornelia is wearing a green dress with a knitted shawl and a gold locket necklace. Her hair is in a fancy bun on her head.

I walk over to them. "Good evening, ladies," I say.

Cornelia waves me off. "We're meeting gentlemen callers here. Roxy said we could bring plus-ones. Have you seen men in suits with ties matching our dresses?"

I frown in complete confusion. "I'm sorry. What?"

"We swiped right on some dates," Margie explains.

I nearly spit out my drink. Somehow, I swallow before asking, "On a dating app?"

"No, on a slot machine," she says with a pointed look.

I hold up a hand in defense. "Sorry. I'm just surprised. I didn't know you all were looking to date."

Cornelia sighs and pats my arm. "Dear boy, we're old, not dead." She smiles. "Look, there they are." She points to two older gentlemen who are in the book section labeled "Billionaire Romance."

"Well, have fun," I say as Cornelia kisses my cheek and Margie pats my arm. I watch them walk over and wonder how I've had trouble wanting to date again but these two widows are ready to mingle. Shaking my head, I turn back to watch the only woman I've considered making mine since Lydia and I broke up.

She's talking with some people that I don't know. Taking a seat on a chair, I watch her as I drink my beer. The crowd is slowly exiting as the evening is coming to an end. After talking with their dates and getting their books signed, Cornelia and Margie and their gentlemen callers leave. And then Carly and Bray followed by Cam and Drew.

"How's it going?" Al's voice comes from next to me as he sits down in the chair on the other side of a small table.

"It's going," I reply.

He leans back. "She did good." I glance over as he looks around. I can see a mix of pride and sadness on his face. It has to be hard being here tonight. I can only imagine this store holds so many memories for him.

"She did do good." I pause. "I think Edith would like it."

"She would. She loved a good romance story," Al says with a faraway smile.

"What's that like?" I ask.

He looks over at me. "What is what like, kid?"

"Being part of a good romance story," I state because he was. Everyone who knew them saw it. They were the real deal.

He gives me a sad smile and leans over. "It was the best. You know, you shouldn't give up on it. The best love stories come knocking when you least expect it. And sometimes, they come from the most unusual places."

We both glance at Roxy. "That they do," I agree as I feel myself itching to touch her for the second time tonight.

"You shouldn't let that one get away, Grayson. She's a

once-in-a-lifetime woman. Trust this old man, he knows." He chuckles as he points to himself.

"You know what, Al? You're right," I state.

"I know." He looks at his watch. "Well, it's past this old man's bedtime." He stands and tips his head at me, giving me a salute as he walks over to Roxy and kisses her cheek before leaving. The signing authors are packing up their things to leave and Roxy's family is saying their goodbyes. Roxy is ever the professional, helping the authors, then the caterer and bartender.

I lean against a wall as I watch everyone pack up. Eventually, it's just Roxy, Jocelyn, and myself.

"You ladies need anything?" I ask as I push off the wall.

"Nah," Jocelyn says as she shuts down the computer, not bothering to look up at me.

"Go ahead home, Joc. I got it from here. I'll see you tomorrow," Roxy says, her eyes meeting mine.

"Oh, uh, OK. We did great tonight, by the way," Jocelyn says.

"Oh?"

"Yep," she says as she grabs a bag from under the desk. "See you tomorrow. Good night, Gray."

"Good night, Joc," I reply. She looks between us, and out of the corner of my eye, I see her roll her eyes.

When it's just Roxy and I, she steps forward. Then I step forward. We meet in the middle of the store.

"You're amazing, you know that," I whisper as my hand comes up to cup her jaw.

She leans her head against my hand. "Say that again."

"You. Are. Amazing," I punctuate each word as I press my lips to hers.

I pull back after a moment because I know what I want. It's crazy. I don't know if it'll make things better or worse, but at this moment, I don't care.

I take her hand in mine and pull her toward the door.

She laughs. "Where are we going?"

"Keys," I state.

She grabs them from under the desk and turns off the lights before locking the door. She follows me to my apartment. I open the door and she steps inside. I watch her dress swish as she walks, and fuck me, I need her in a way that I've never needed a woman.

I walk toward her, caging her against a wall and putting a hand on either side of her head. I run my nose along the long line of her neck and then her jaw. Her breath hitches.

"If you don't want this, leave now," I say as I pull one hand away, letting her have an out because if she stays, I want her, all of her.

"I want this," she whispers in a barely audible voice.

I smirk. "Thank fucking God!" I growl as I bend down and hoist her over my shoulder, carrying her into my bedroom.

CHAPTER TWENTY-ONE

Roxy

I squeal as I reach for anything, which ends up being Gray's ass. Fuck. This man has a great ass. Gray is tall. I know this because I'm not exactly short and he towers over me by a good five inches at least.

When we're in his bedroom, he slowly lets me slide down his body. We stand chest to chest, our breaths coming out ragged as we look at each other.

"Is this actually happening?" I ask because my mind has gone blank, and I don't know what else to say.

"It is so fucking happening," he says in a strained voice as if he's holding back.

All of a sudden, I'm feeling...bashful.

"What?" Gray asks, his hand coming up to grip my chin, keeping me from looking away.

"I...wasn't planning on doing this today," I admit.

"So?" he says as his brows furrow.

My cheeks heat. "I...I mean, normally if I was going to

hook up with someone, I'd get waxed, bring condoms, you know...all the stuff."

Gray leans down and presses a kiss to my jaw, my neck, and then my clavicle. "Roxy, do you think I care about any of that?"

"Uh, you should care about that condom part," I say with a moan as he nips my shoulder after sliding my dress strap off it.

"I have some," he says, motioning to a nightstand while continuing to kiss a path down my chest to my right breast.

"Oh." I'm silent because now I'm wondering how often he hooks up with women.

As if reading my mind, he brings his face back to mine. "I bought a box to take with me to Vegas after Lydia and I broke up. Hutch, Bray, and Kasen decided I needed to let loose. Only, it felt weird, and I never ended up using any of them."

"Don't condoms, like, expire?" I ask.

"They're still good. It's been less than a year," he explains as he presses a light kiss to my lips.

"I have an IUD. My boyfriend talked me into it. While he was cheating on me with my ex-friend," I say dryly.

"It was with your friend? Damn! He's an idiot," Gray replies in between kisses. "And so is your ex-friend."

"Yeah. They both are," I agree, remembering all the nights I spent crying over at Tay's apartment. I should call her tomorrow and tell her how the soft opening went. Go figure my one and only friend doesn't even live near me anymore.

Gray spins me around and unzips my dress. I kick off my heels as the dress falls to the floor, leaving me in only a strapless bra and panties. He makes quick work of the bra. It lands on the dress.

I hear Gray's clothes moving as he begins to unbutton his shirt. I turn. "Let me," I insist.

His hands fall to his sides, and I slowly unbutton the remaining buttons. I take my time, wanting to savor the moment of unwrapping him as if he's a precious gift.

I push back the white fabric. I've seen him in the hot tub and without his shirt on, so I know he's gorgeous, but it's different now that I can touch him like this. I trail my finger over his pectoral muscles that jump under my touch. Then, even more cautiously, I outline each of his abdominal muscles. How is this man so sculpted?

My fingers brush against the line of hair that disappears into his pants. I run my knuckles over the belt.

He unbuckles it and slides it out quickly and I nearly come on the spot.

"What?" he asks.

"That's hot as fuck. Like book boyfriend hot," I state.

"Taking off my belt is hot?" he questions.

I nod and grin. "Very hot."

"I'll have to remember that for next time," he says as he unzips his pants. He pushes them down and takes his socks and shoes off, leaving us both only in our underwear.

"Are we still faking?" I whisper because I need to be certain. I'm catching feelings for this man, and I need to protect myself.

"I won't hurt you," he promises. Shit. How is Gray so inside my head?

I blow out a breath. "Answer the question, Gray."

He takes my hand and places it over his heart. I feel the thudding beneath his skin. "Does this feel fake?"

I swallow hard and shake my head. "No."

Then, he moves my hand down, sliding our hands beneath the band of his underwear. His fingers intertwine with mine as we grip his erection. "Does this feel fake?"

I roll my eyes at him. "No, but that has nothing to do with faking a relationship."

He leans in and kisses me again. A full soul-shattering kiss that takes my breath away. When he pulls back abruptly, I lean forward, wanting more.

"Does that feel fake?" he says in a raspy voice.

I shake my head again because this time, I'm too stunned to speak.

"Nothing about this is fake anymore, Roxy. I tried. I tried not to feel anything for you. I...don't know if I can do this properly. There's a lot you don't know. But I can't fight my feelings for you anymore. I want to; God, do I want to. For your sake and mine. But I can't. I'm not that strong," he whispers, his eyes searching mine.

My breath comes out as a shudder this time. "I don't want us to hurt each other."

He leans his forehead against mine. "Me either, but I don't think that's a promise we should make right now. There's too much we still need to tell each other. I wish I was a stronger man. I wish I didn't need to know what it felt like to be buried inside you."

"Then, don't wait," I state because I'm losing my mind. His hands have been roaming over my naked flesh and it's driving me insane. At this point, I'd agree to a fake relationship fuck if it meant his dick got to be inside me.

Our lips crash together and then we're pushing each other's underwear down before we fall onto the bed with a bounce. I scoot up to the pillows on my back and he follows as he kisses his way down my body. His nose runs along the inside of my thigh before he plants a soft kiss just above my folds.

"I've been wanting to do this for days," he says as his thumbs separate my most intimate skin and his tongue circles my clit. My head falls back against the pillows as I moan.

His tongue is soon accompanied by one finger and then two. The man is straight-up playing me like one of his instruments and damn him if he isn't a fucking maestro.

My hands involuntarily find his head as my hips rise off the bed, seeking more, needing more. He presses a hand on my hip to keep me flat as his tongue licks around where his fingers penetrate me and then back up to my clit. As he pulses it against my bundle of nerves and his fingers curl deep inside, I feel myself start to unravel.

"Don't stop," I command, my hands gripping his head tightly. "Please, don't stop."

As much as I pegged Grayson Porter as a "never take a command" type of alpha male, he surprises me and continues doing exactly what I need him to do. It takes less than thirty seconds for me to detonate around his fingers. He slows his movements until he's still. He leaves his fingers inside me for a long moment. When I open my eyes, he's watching where his fingers are. Finally, he pulls them free and licks them clean before leaning over me and opening a drawer on his nightstand.

He tosses three condoms on the bed. I look up at him with a raised eyebrow.

"Oh, wifey, one time is not going to be nearly enough," he offers as he grabs one condom and rips open the foil packet.

"Let me," I insist as I take the protection from him. He sits on his haunches between my legs and I sit up, stroking him from tip to base. He groans and closes his eyes for a brief second. Now that I can see him, all of him, I know he's perfect. He's tall and muscled, but not bulky. He has body hair but not too much. His dick...well, if I had an adult toy created just for me, I think I'd have it sculpted after his member because it's literally exactly what I'd dream up as the perfect penis. It's long, but not too long; thick, but not too thick; and shaped with just a little arc to it that I know will hit me exactly how I need it to.

I lean forward and press a kiss to the slit on the crown of his perfect dick. And then I slide my tongue down the length.

He grabs my hair at the base of my neck, and I look up at him with my lips sealed around the tip of his cock.

"Fuck, Roxy. You have no idea how fucking sexy you look with your lips wrapped around me. But I need to be inside you, right now," he growls.

I release him with a pop, and he groans. Slowly, I slide the condom down his length and lean back onto the pillow. He takes his erection in his hand and slides it up and down my wetness until I think I might burst from need. And again, as if reading my mind, he slides into me in one long stroke as we both release our breath.

CHAPTER TWENTY-TWO

Grayson

Fuck. Roxy's inner muscles grip me hard as I try to move. The only thing making it possible is the crazy amount of wetness that aids me in gliding in and out. I take it slow, even when her hips buck against me. I'm savoring it; savoring her. And damn, she feels good.

I look down at where our bodies are joined, and I have to close my eyes so I don't come too fast. I breathe deeply and begin to move, feeling her heat each time I press inside her.

My hands grip her hips, holding on and guiding her as she thrusts up to meet me. When I finally feel under control, I open my eyes and gaze down at this incredible woman. A fierce possessiveness I've never felt before begins to wash over me like a rogue wave. I'm sinking beneath its gravitational pull, and I don't want to get back up. I want to stay here, buried inside her, our gazes locked and our bodies as close as they can be. We're in our own private universe.

I start moving faster. Normally, I want to change positions over and over until I'm pulled over the edge, but not tonight, not with her. I like her beneath me. I like the feel of her smooth skin under mine.

We begin to move in sync. It's like our bodies know each other even though we're still learning.

"Keep going. I'm so close," she moans.

"I got you, baby," I whisper as I move faster, thrusting upward so my pelvic bone grinds against her clit with each stroke. Then I reach between us and circle it.

"Yes!" she cries out and I start to feel her muscles clenching in waves around my dick.

"Fuck!" I roar as Roxy's orgasm carries me over the edge with her into an abyss of pleasure.

I lean over her, keeping myself suspended as my cock jerks a few last times. I'm about to lean down to kiss her when out of nowhere, Licorice jumps up on the bed, sticks her head between Roxy and me, and lets out the loudest meow that I've ever heard.

Roxy looks at me and I look at her and we burst into laughter. I pull out and dispose of the condom while Roxy snuggles the kitten.

"What's wrong, little lady?" she coos. Licorice's purr intensifies, and when I lie down next to them, she stretches out one long paw and places it on my arm.

"Someone doesn't like not being the center of her father's attention," Roxy says with a giggle.

I place a hand on Licorice's back and stroke her warm, soft fur. "Licorice, I hate to break it to you, but your mom and I have a busy night planned. So you're going to have to find something else to do."

I go to take her away from Roxy but Roxy puts up her hand. "You can't move her yet. She's being so cute," she protests before she leans down to kiss Licorice's head.

"No way. She needs to go. I am not done with you yet," I grumble.

Roxy laughs and leans over to kiss my cheek. "We have all night."

My phone pings with a text and I roll over to check it. My heart sinks as I see a text from my mother.

Egg Donor: We're having a birthday dinner for your father on the twenty-second. Let me know if you can't attend.

Groaning, I toss my phone back on the nightstand.

"What's that about?" Roxy asks as Licorice suddenly wakes and runs off to have her nightly ritual of zoomies all over my apartment before passing out in some weird spot like in the kitchen sink, half on the arm of a chair, or curled up on my robot vacuum.

I lean my head back on the pillow and stare up at the ceiling. "That was my mother. Apparently, she's having a party for my dad on the twenty-second. And my attendance is expected."

Roxy rolls to her side and I glance over at her. "I can go. I mean, if you want me to go."

I roll on my side, and we stare at each other. "You want to meet my family?" I ask.

She nods. "I mean, you met my family tonight."

"Yes, but your family is...normal," I point out. And they were normal, albeit very smart and accomplished but normal. They didn't say condescending things or badmouth her. They all seemed supportive. I know Roxy has a chip on her shoulder about not being as accomplished as her siblings, but I didn't see any red flags.

"Can I ask you something?" I add as I search her eyes.

"Sure."

"Why do you feel inadequate compared to your siblings? I mean, I get they've done a lot in their lives, but so have you,"

I state because it's true and I can't figure out why she doesn't see it.

Roxy rolls onto her back. She's quiet for a moment and I think she's not going to answer me, but then she does.

"My siblings were all in the gifted and talented program in school. They took AP classes and my older sister even graduated a year early. I was just...normal. I took normal classes. I got normal grades. I did normal activities. I wasn't an overachiever, and no, my family never said I sucked, but I just... teachers would say things and my friends. I once went on a date with a guy who just wanted to meet Cybil. Anyhow, I guess, I hid away in books because it was something that took me away from my inner thoughts, an escape. This store is the first time I've felt like I even belong in my family," she explains and then turns her head to look at me. "It's silly, isn't it?"

"No. It's not," I assure her.

"Anyhow, after the guy thing with Cybil, I just decided not to be serious with anyone until I met Richard at the end of college. We dated close to a year. It was the longest time I had ever been with anyone. And then, he asked me to move in with him. Things were good at first, and then I came home early and my friend Nikki was...well, let's just say she wasn't sucking on a popsicle," she says with a grimace.

I reach over and cup her cheek, kissing her for a moment. "I'm sorry that happened. You deserved better."

"Thank you. At least I have my other friend, Tay. She and my family really helped me move on afterward," she whispers. She's quiet for a beat before turning to me. "What about you?"

"What about me?"

She gives me a pointed look. "Your dating life."

"Oh." Now it's my turn to be quiet. Fuck it. She's bound to find out eventually. "Like I said before, I had a girlfriend in high school. We broke up when we went to college. And then I dated a few women, one of them for about six months. After college, I was sort of sowing my wild oats and then I met a woman through my dad's friend. We dated pretty seriously for four years. Three years into our relationship, I decided I didn't want to work for my parents' business. I had studied music in college. My parents thought it was a phase." I make quotation marks. "But I never stopped. My girlfriend acted all supportive, but a year after I moved in here, she told me I needed to get back to reality if we were going to be together. We had a big fight about it, and we broke up."

"You broke up because you wanted to pursue a music career?" she asks, her eyes looking sad.

"Yep," I reply as I search her eyes. She looks genuinely mad.

"What a bitch!" she snarls, and I laugh.

"Lydia was just...she's rich, she wants a rich husband. And music isn't exactly lucrative," I say, motioning around us. Not that one-eleven Hearts Lane is a bad building, it's just not the insanely posh condo I previously had complete with a doorman, secured elevators, and amenities like an indoor pool and full gym. It's also not right in the city center. I remember Lydia scoffing at the building as if she'd catch a disease entering it.

"So, you dated a snob," Roxy states.

"I dated a woman accustomed to a certain lifestyle," I correct her because my little sister is drastically different aside from the fact that she's never once made a comment about my music career or where I live. My parents, on the other hand, well, they side with Lydia.

Roxy rolls her eyes. "Yeah, she sounds like a real fucking gem."

"I think you're a real fucking gem," I tease, wanting to change the subject because all this talk about my ex is bringing me down. I pull her to me and roll us over, so I hover over her gorgeous body as my eyes look down and back up again. Damn, I owe Al a drink for setting us up.

"You're drooling," she says smugly. I grin. I like this side of Roxy when she's strong-willed and playful. I find it hard to marry with her insecure side but put the two together and she's just...well, I'm beginning to think she's pretty damn near perfect.

"I guess I should eat something," I whisper as I start trailing kisses down her body.

Her hands fly to my hair. Fuck, I love when she tugs on it. I line up with her wet heat and lick my lips.

"Did you read that in a book at my store?" she says, as I run my tongue through her slit and she draws in a sharp breath.

"No, but it sounds like I have some homework to do," I chuckle against her swollen flesh. If finding hot lines in those romance books is a way to my woman's heart, it looks like I'm about to start a book club with the guys. Maybe they could use some tips as well.

CHAPTER TWENTY-THREE

Roxy

Why am I so nervous? I take a deep, steadying breath for the third time in a minute.

Gray's hand leaves his stick shift and comes to rest over mine. "Relax. You are a beautiful and successful business-woman. They will love you."

I give him side-eye. Why is he so calm? It's been nearly three weeks since we started dating for real. Although we've only been together for a month and a half, if we count our fake-dating time, I feel like we've been together forever. For a man who left such a bad first impression, Gray has proven he's actually a charming, sexy-as-fuck, intelligent, and thoughtful boyfriend. And the sex...is...well, he wasn't joking about reading all my favorite steamy romance novels and he most definitely took notes.

He's been extra attentive this week because my official grand opening is only a little over a week away, although I've been contemplating pushing it back. I've been on edge and he offered to cancel our attendance at his father's birthday party, but I assured him I'd be fine. However, now that we're almost at his parents' home, I'm having serious second thoughts.

My leg bounces as I nervously look at the enormous mansions on this tree-lined street. Gray's hand grips my thigh.

"I can turn around," he assures me. I glance over at him and shake my head. "I don't like it when my wifey is nervous."

His use of the ridiculous nickname makes my lips twitch into a smile. He grins back at me as he pulls up to a house... strike that, an enormous French-manor-house/castle-looking building. When Gray said his father owned an investment firm, I figured they would have a nice home, but this...isn't a home...it's an estate.

My eyes widen further as he pulls into a circular drive with a working fountain in the middle of it. Small solar lights line the driveway. The sun is just getting low in the sky, but it's bright enough to see the rainbow of perfectly manicured shrubs, flowers, and lawn.

"Where's the gatehouse?" I mutter, mostly to myself.

He chuckles. "I should warn you. The staff miss me. Particularly Leopold, our head of staff," he states as if every family has a freaking person running their household.

He parks the car and walks around it, opening my door and offering me his hand. I accept it and he pulls me to my feet and against his warm, toned body. He plants a gentle kiss on my lips. "You are better than anyone you will meet in this house tonight. Don't forget that."

I start to nod, but the enormous wooden front doors open. If I thought Pierce and Haven's lake house was extra, it pales in comparison to what awaits me inside this home.

"Come on," Gray urges me, his voice laced with amusement as he presses his palm to my lower back and ushers me toward an older gentleman at the door. I know it's not his father because even though Gray doesn't have a single photo of them in his home, Jocelyn and I internet stalked him. I've even seen his ex.

"Leopold, this is my girlfriend, Roxy," Gray introduces as he walks up to Leopold and hugs him.

"It's nice to meet you," Leopold says extending a hand to me. I'm half-expecting a British accent and am mildly disappointed when he has a strong New England accent.

We shake and I suddenly feel timid. "Nice to meet you too," I manage as my hand drops away and I take in my opulent surroundings. Crystal chandeliers, silk-patterned wallpaper, priceless pieces of art, and stone that probably cost more than my entire apartment building surround us.

"This way," Leopold says as he walks down a long corridor.

We follow and Gray leans toward me. "The less you say, the better," he suggests.

I frown. Is he embarrassed by me? What about the pep talk he just gave me?

Before I can ask, we're at double doors that are at least seven feet high. Leopold opens one and motions for us to enter. With a hand pressed to my lower back, Gray leads me inside a formal dining room. A table easily capable of seating twenty people fills the center of the space. It sits upon a woven rug that I assume is antique and foreign. The chairs are dark wood and intricately carved. And a tablecloth made of silk covers the table. It perfectly matches the paint on the walls. A large floral arrangement sits in the center of the table.

There are several people already seated. A man at the head of the table with the same blue eyes as Gray who, based on photos I saw online, is his father. His mother sits diagonally from him. Her hair looks perfect as if she just came from a salon. His sister sits next to her.

But it's the woman sitting across from his mother that has

my breath catching. She looks like a model. She rises from her chair, focusing her gaze on Gray as she seemingly ignores my presence. She's tall, even taller than me, and graceful, and makes me look like the ugly duckling.

Lydia.

Gray's ex-girlfriend is at this family dinner. What. The. Fuck?

I glance over at Gray. He looks...confused.

The room is silent for way too many seconds. It's Lydia who breaks the trance.

"Gray! It's so good to see you," she says warmly in a voice that sounds like she's a villain in a cartoon film. She sounds sincere in the fakest way possible.

She walks over and places her hand on his shoulder as she leans in and kisses his cheek.

"What are you doing here, Lydia?" Gray says, his voice low and menacing. He looks ready to punch a wall. I can see his jaw pulsing as he speaks. His hand is still on the small of my back and I feel it vibrate with anger. Oh shit. This family dinner thing is going to end in epic fireworks and not the good kind, more like the kind that happens when a fireworks factory catches fire, abrupt and too intense.

"Oh, uh, your parents insisted I join. I didn't want to miss the opportunity to congratulate you on your latest film venture," she says with a smile that is as fake as her voice. She might look gorgeous, but it's clear after ten seconds of hearing her speak that the beauty is only skin deep.

"Thank you," he mutters, his voice staying evenly toned, his only tell being his clenching jaw. Although, I swear there's a vein beginning to emerge in his forehead.

I watch them look at each other and I wonder what unspoken words are passing between them. Does he miss her? I feel my nostrils flare as jealousy begins to course through my veins. She left him. He should be way more livid. He should be screaming and putting on a spectacle as he tells his family we are leaving, but no, he's silent.

"Gray, darling, please be seated with your friend and introduce us," his mother says, giving me a fake smile that rivals Lydia's. Lovely, a table of fake people. The irony that Gray and I started out as a fake couple is not lost on me as I walk up to a chair and take a seat, deciding to play the super sweet and classy girlfriend.

"It's so nice to meet you all. I'm Roxy Benedict, Gray's girlfriend," I state as I place a napkin on my lap. I can feel Gray walking behind me and taking a seat as Lydia sits on his other side.

I almost feel as if I'm watching a movie instead of my life. While I'm having some weird out-of-body experience, Gray's father begins to speak.

"I didn't realize you were bringing a plus-one," he says dryly. "So I took the liberty of inviting Lydia. You two should talk after dinner."

Wonderful. This is just great. I half expect him to add one of those villain *hahaha*s after his words, but he just motions to a woman at the door to bring food. The woman and two others set silver plates with little domes on them on the table, while a man sets salad plates in front of each of us. The staff quickly add a place setting for me as well.

Gray's sister has been sitting silent, but her eyes stay trained on me. "So, Roxy, I hear you own a bookstore," she says quietly before taking a bite of her salad, adding, "I'm Adriana, Gray's sister, by the way. It's nice to meet you." She levels her stare at her father before returning to mine with a smile, a real one. OK, so one of his family members seems to be normal. Promising.

"Uh, yes. I just opened it," I state.

"Oh, that's so sweet. A small business. Just like the

movies," Lydia says with a smirk that I want to slap right off her smug face.

"It's quite impressive. You should all visit it," Gray says before taking a bite of salad.

"So, son, tell us about this deal with Pierce. How much will you be making?" his father asks, seemingly ignoring me as if I'm the hired help. How in the hell did Gray spawn from these people?

My family is kind and supportive. And as I sit there and listen to Gray talk about his film deal, I realize for the first time how lucky I am. His family questions everything he says. They are awful. Yes, my siblings are all super accomplished and smart, and yes, I have a big old chip on my shoulder, but they have never once judged me. Even when I had to move back home after my breakup, penniless and with no real career, no one said a word about it. They just opened their arms to me like they always do. As the dinner continues, his family ignores me aside from occasional smiles from his sister, I begin to realize how wrong I've been about my own family. How have I been so blind? And Gray is right, my business is impressive. I've accomplished that with very little help from anyone else, and after hitting an all-time low. I'm a phoenix and I've risen from my ashes. Shit. That is impressive.

"Dessert will be served on the veranda," the woman in a kitchen uniform says from the door.

I realize our meal is over. A meal including filet mignon and lobster tails. I wanted so badly to refer to it as surf and turf, but I had a distinct feeling that wouldn't help the situation.

Everyone rises from their chairs.

"Where's the bathroom?" I whisper to Gray as I follow him out into the hallway. He motions to a door.

"I'll just be outside," he says as he points to a room to our right where giant sliding walls open onto a patio that over-looks a vista view of the lake. I hadn't realized how close we were to it.

I nod and excuse myself as I go into the bathroom. It's enormous, like the size of my apartment. There is a basket filled with fresh hand towels and a basket to drop them in when finished. It's like the fancy bathrooms at the country club where my dad plays golf. That's probably the only time I've seen something like that.

With an eye roll, I walk out and head toward the back deck. I see Gray's parents talking with their daughter, but I don't see Gray and I don't see Lydia. A shiver runs over me.

"Gray and Lydia just took a walk to see my new rose garden," his mother says as she notices me standing and looking around. She motions toward the path leading to a hedged area off to the side of the house.

"Oh," I state because I don't know what else to say. I step down onto the path and follow it, hearing some whispered words as I approach.

When I reach a clearing, I peer inside it and my heart stops. Gray is kissing Lydia.

I gasp and they pull apart. Gray turns to me, his face paling. "Roxy, it's not what you think."

Memories of Richard saying those exact words to me fill my mind and I feel tears threaten. I spin on my heels and head straight up the path and to the veranda.

"Thank you for a lovely evening. I'm not feeling well, so I'm going to duck out early," I say to them.

"Oh dear," his mother says but she doesn't actually seem concerned.

"I'll just see myself out. I can call a car. I don't want to pull Grayson away from all of you early," I say as I turn to the sliding wall that's still open. I walk through it and pull up an app to summon a car.

"Ms. Benedict?" Leopold's voice comes from the hallway.

"Not feeling well, I'm calling a car," I say to him as I hurry to the front door.

"I'll open the gate," he says, referring to the black gate at the bottom of their driveway. He opens the door for me and I practically run through it.

"Roxy!" I hear Gray's voice and I have to blink back tears.

Leopold holds the door for Gray and Gray runs out into the driveway.

"Wait! Please!" Gray yells as he runs to catch up with me.

I take a deep breath and turn to him. "Go back inside, Grayson. I'm going home," I hiss from behind clenched teeth as I glance at my rideshare app to confirm the car is approaching.

"Roxy, it's not what you think. Lydia kissed me. I didn't kiss her. She thought she could reconnect with me tonight. But that's not possible. Because I'm already with you, I'm falling for you," he says, his voice pleading.

"No, stop. We are *not* doing this. I can't do this again," I whisper as I fight the tears that threaten me once more.

The car pulls up and I open the door. "We're done," I say quietly as I get inside.

"Roxy!" he calls out. I see him reach for his phone as the car pulls away and I block his number. I can't do this. Not again. Not now. Not ever.

CHAPTER TWENTY-FOUR

Grayson

"Dude, come on! If I'm going to hang that trail cam high enough to make sure the trash pandas don't get to it, I need your help," Hutch pleads as he nurses a beer.

I sigh for the tenth time in as many minutes. "I don't have time right now. Maybe next week."

"Any word from Kasen?" Hutch asks Al.

"No." Al pauses. "Where's Roxy?" he asks, looking around at our neighbors who have slowly trickled upstairs for happy hour despite the rain.

Carly comes stomping toward me and pokes her finger on my chest. "You know, you're a real jerk. I thought you were better than that," she seethes.

I put my hands up in the air. "What are you talking about?"

She rolls her eyes and taps her foot. Bray looks at her and then at me. "You're in big trouble."

I glare at him and then look back at Carly. "Roxy told me what you did."

"I didn't *do* anything," I mutter. "It was a misunderstanding."

Cam walks up and stands next to Carly, folding her arms over her chest.

"Oh? Did your tongue just fall into Lydia's mouth by mistake?" she asks with a raised eyebrow.

Everyone falls silent and looks at me. By now, most of them had figured out we were really dating.

"Lydia kissed me. And as I pushed away, Roxy happened to find us," I explain as calmly as I can muster.

"Right. 'Cause it's so easy to accidentally lean all the way up and kiss you," Cam says with a glare.

"For fuck's sake, I didn't kiss Lydia. I hate Lydia. After Roxy left, I had a big fight with her and told her to fucking leave my parents' home. Then I had a big fight with my parents and left," I state. I don't mention how my mom screamed at me for ruining my dad's birthday dinner or how Adriana tried to side with me and my dad told her to shut up and how I practically punched him for talking to my sister that way. It was bad. Lydia just stood by and then tried to hug me, but I stormed out of there before I made an even bigger mistake.

"Does Pierce know about your relationship situation?" Cam asks and I suddenly feel panicked. Pierce knows nothing. For all intents and purposes, he thinks we're still together and have been together.

"Pierce isn't part of this situation," I say as I stand because I don't need this shit from my friends right now.

Cam smirks and my stomach drops. "What?" I ask.

"Jocelyn spilled the beans," she says. Then I see her look a little sorry. "Sorry, Gray. I know you were trying to make a good impression with him."

I pause mid-step and stare at her. "What do you mean?"

She pats my shoulder. "Haven, his wife, came by the store this afternoon, and uh, well, Jocelyn thought you guys had told her the truth since it was all real...it was real, right?"

I groan. "Yes. What did she say exactly?"

Cam bites her lip and then releases it. "She said you guys had been real dating after starting fake dating and then she said you had fake dated to impress Pierce."

The blood drains from my face. "What?" I whisper.

"Uh, yeah. I just happened to be in the store picking Drew and me up some books we'd ordered. So I heard every-thing," she says with a sheepish look.

"What did Roxy say?" I ask.

"Oh, Roxy wasn't there. She had to pick up packages from the post office," Cam explains.

Carly nods. "That's when I walked in to see if Cam was able to make me a latte before I picked up Ava from her after-school program."

"So Roxy doesn't know this happened?" I ask.

They both shrug.

"Damn it! I told her to tell Jocelyn not to say anything. Just like I told you guys," I say with a huff as I rub the bridge of my nose.

"Well, message not received," Cam says. "Sorry, Gray."

"What are you sorry for, dear?" Margie asks as she steps out of the stairwell with Cornelia in tow.

"Jocelyn broke the fake-relationship news to Pierce's wife," Cam yells over her shoulder.

"Well, fuck a duck! That's no good," Margie says as she walks over to me and pats my arm. "What can we do?"

"Where's Roxy?" I growl.

"Closing up the store," Carly says as Ava walks over from where she was sitting at the table under the umbrella and coloring something.

"What does fuck a duck mean, Mommy?" she asks.

Cornelia whacks Margie on the back of the head. And Margie mouths, "Sorry."

Carly rolls her eyes. "It's grown-up talk, sweetie. Why don't you go back to coloring?"

"Will you color with me, Unca Bray?" she asks, giving him a pathetic puppy dog look.

"Of course, little nugget. Lead the way," he says as he gives me a look that says, "Sorry, dude."

I turn back and motion to Al to pour me a double of scotch. He does and I down it in one gulp before turning to Cam and Carly.

"What exactly did she say to Haven?" I question as I look between them.

"Uh, well, Haven asked if Roxy was there," Cam starts, "and Jocelyn said she had gone to the post office and would be back soon. And then Haven said that she was going to see if they could all go out to dinner this week because she just finished a book and would love to have Roxy there to debrief on it." Cam closes her eyes for a moment as if trying hard to remember.

"That's when I walked closer," Carly says. "Jocelyn then said that it's a good thing they are really dating now because it'll be a lot easier to go out on the date."

I slap my forehead. "She seriously said that?"

Cam nods. "Yeah, something like that. I think Jocelyn knew she fucked up though because she got really pale. Haven was like, what do you mean? And Jocelyn was like, oh, haha, they weren't really together at first. And then she said, I think Gray said he had a girlfriend and Roxy said she'd play along, but one thing led to another and...well, it's all real now."

"Oh my God, I need another," I say as I blindly hand Al my glass.

"It's fine. Haven laughed and said that's adorable and to let Roxy know that she stopped by. And Jocelyn said I will. She's been in a foul mood today and that will probably make her feel better," Cam adds.

My jaw involuntarily clenches at that statement. "So she hasn't told Jocelyn about our fight?"

"I guess not. We both saw her as we left. She was coming up the sidewalk with a box and looked...well, not happy, so we stopped, and eventually, she told us what happened, but Jocelyn was still inside the store," Carly explains.

I let out a long breath. "OK. I need to go talk to her," I say as I slam my latest drink and start back toward the stairs.

"Gray, don't do anything rash, man!" Hutch yells after me. But it's too late. I'm riled as fuck. It's one thing that she won't listen to me about what happened with Lydia. It's another that she's not telling Jocelyn to stay quiet about the whole fake-relationship thing.

I make it down all seven flights of stairs in record time and run out the door and right into her store. Her head pops up from the desk and looks at me before sighing.

"What do you want?" she asks harshly.

"I want to know why the fuck you didn't tell Jocelyn to keep her trap shut about our relationship situation," I growl as I point a finger at her.

Her face goes red and she stands, walking straight up to me. "For your information, I just found out what she said. I hadn't bothered telling her because I didn't know Haven would come by, and also, I was going to tell her we aren't even together anymore but then I had to go deal with something at the post office. And you know what, fuck you! I'm not the one who was caught cheating!"

Now, I feel heat creeping into my face. "I wasn't cheating!" I yell. "If you would freaking listen for one damn minute, you'd know that as soon as I walked into the garden that my mother told me to look at, Lydia jumped me. If you had waited two seconds, you would have seen me push her away and yell at her, but you were too sure of what you saw. You have zero trust in me. In fact, you have massive trust issues in addition to the whole self-esteem thing. You should go sort that out, Roxy. Now, I have to go talk with freaking Pierce and sort this out and hope I don't get fired from the one effing gig that I've worked my ass to get. So, thanks a lot."

"You know what? First impressions are really correct," she seethes.

I glare at her. "That's not what you were saying two nights ago," I say and immediately regret it. Her face falls and I can see the hurt and I fucking want to punch myself for saying it.

"Get. Out," she manages from behind her clenched jaw.

"Roxy, I..." I trail off because if looks could kill, I'd be dead. "OK, I'm leaving," I say calmly as I hold up my hands.

"Good. And don't come back, ever! And good luck being a single cat dad!" she screams.

Something about that hits my heart and makes me lose my temper. "I won't come back and you'll never see Licorice again. She doesn't need a mom that jumps to conclusions and then doesn't hold up her end of a bargain."

"Right, like she needs a dad who is accusatory and cheats on her mom," she retorts.

"I'm out of here," I say as I wave her off and stomp out of the store. As soon as I'm back in my apartment, regret starts to seep through me again. But my anger won't let me go apologize. So instead, I feed Licorice and start to compose a song. I need to calm down before I talk to Pierce. I need to figure out what to say and I haven't a clue.

CHAPTER TWENTY-FIVE

Roxy

"Wow. Uh, nice shirt," Carly says as she walks into my store. I'm wearing a shirt that says "Men suck. Except Book Boyfriends." It was a silly gift from Isla when Richard and I broke up, but it seems appropriate today.

"Thanks," I say dryly as I reach for my cup of coffee.

"So..." Carly begins as she leans against the desk. "Did you see Hutch is putting up a new motion camera? He somehow talked Bray into helping him. I sort of wish they'd just let it stay a mystery, you know?"

Shrugging, I set my mug down. "Why do they care so much, anyhow?"

"Hutch is just...well, frankly he's obsessed with it. I think he's using it as an escape from his reality. Poor guy has been through a lot these past few years with his injury, some girl troubles, and his mom was sick."

I frown. Now I feel like a jerk. I had no idea Hutch had gone through so much.

"That's too bad," I state. "Hey, speaking of mysteries, has anyone talked to Kasen yet?"

She shakes her head. "No, but Al assured me again the other day that Kasen is fine. I still don't get why he just doesn't tell us what is going on, but he's all quiet about it." She rolls her eyes. "I sort of want to kick Kasen's ass when he does come home. I worry about him. I know he's this big old badass and all, but you can't run from life forever."

"I suppose," I agree as I look past Carly and see Jocelyn talking to Hutch.

Carly follows my gaze. "What do you make of that?" she asks.

"Jocelyn's a flirt. She flirts with, like, every guy that comes in here. I can't get a read on whether she's actually interested in any of them, or if that is just innately who she is," I admit.

"I think they have a crush on each other," Carly declares as she crosses her arms and continues to watch them. "I mean, look at that body language. He's leaning down to talk to her. She's leaning in toward him. It's a total unequivocal sign of desire."

I giggle. "I never say this to customers, but I think you might be reading too many romance novels."

"Hell no! Drew just finished that one you recommended and I'm starting it tonight. I'm not swearing off them. Shit, it's the only stress reliever I have right now."

I smile at her. "Well then, let me introduce you to your next billionaire book boyfriend," I offer as I point her in the direction of one of my favorite books in her favorite romance genre.

"Well, thanks for the book rec. I gotta go run an errand before I pick up Ava. I swear, I wish I had a billionaire for real so that I could send a driver to get her some days. I love my daughter, but doing this alone is...a lot sometimes," she says with a sigh.

"I'm sure it is, but you do a great job," I encourage as I walk her to the door.

"I don't know. I hope I'm doing a good enough job. She's a good kiddo, you know?"

I grin because I'm remembering Ava schooling Al on maraschino cherries the other night. Like what kid knows about that? "She's the best. If I ever have a kid, I hope she's half as cool as Ava."

Carly laughs as she opens the door. "If your future kid is anything like you, she'll be awesome. I mean, look around, how could she not be?"

I'm not sure why her words hit me hard, but damn, I can't help but believe them as I look around at my store. She might be right.

"See ya," she calls out as she leaves me looking at everything I created.

A moment later, the door opens and my head swivels to find Jocelyn standing there, staring at me.

"What?" I ask, looking down to see if I dribbled coffee on my new blue top.

"You look...happy? Proud? Don't know, but I like it on you," Jocelyn says with a wink as she walks over to the desk and sits down in front of a computer where she's been ordering some books.

"Joc?" I start as I sit down next to her.

"Yep," she replies without looking up at me.

"Did you, uh, tell Haven that Gray and I were fake dating?" I ask.

Jocelyn freezes. "Oh, fuck. I'm so sorry. I thought...since you all were, like, real dating...oh no, how bad is it?" she stammers as her head whips toward me.

"It's alright. Gray was upset. I guess someone said something about it," I explain.

She smacks her forehead. "I'm such an idiot. I assumed

Gray told them when you all decided to real date. I mean, it's a pretty good story."

"I guess it is...or was, whatever," I mutter.

She frowns and pushes her chair back so she's facing me. "What do you mean, was?"

I look around us, noting the last browsing customer who waves and heads out of the store. When we are alone, I turn back to her and tell her all about the crazy dinner at Gray's parents' home and our little fight about Pierce finding out we weren't actually dating.

"Whoa! I mean, I'm sorry about the Pierce thing, totally my idiotic fault, but he *kissed* his ex in front of you!" she yells.

"Chill. And he didn't exactly know I was there behind him. But yes, he did," I say. I feel my eyes burning and I blink back the tears.

"Damn. I really thought he was one of the good ones," Jocelyn says with a sigh.

"Me too," I reply sadly as I play with a loose thread on the hem of my top. Was I really that wrong about Gray? He seemed so...right. He wasn't anything like Richard. Or, at least I didn't think he was. Ugh! I hate this. Why can't I have a romance like in a novel? Hell, I'd take one half as good as in a novel. No, fuck it, I deserve the novel. I deserve the grand gesture. I deserve more than a man who doesn't trust me and kisses his ex.

I'm about to say this when the door chime goes off. I look over to see Margie and Cornelia.

"Hello, ladies," I say, hoping I sound cheerful and not like the angry woman I am.

Margie pokes Cornelia in the ribs and they walk over to us. "What's wrong?" Margie asks.

Well, shit, guess I'm easier to see through than I thought.

"Oh nothing, just a little fight with Gray," I brush off my true feelings with the little white lie.

Jocelyn rolls her eyes. "He was kissing his ex."

Margie's eyes widen and Cornelia's narrow. "That little fucker," Cornelia hisses. "Was it Lydia?"

Too shocked to answer, I simply nod.

"She's a money-hungry, little hussy. Are you sure he wanted to kiss her? Because last I checked that woman nearly gutted Gray," Cornelia states.

"I mean, I saw them kissing. Gray took me to his parents' home for dinner and she was there. They went to the garden and I saw them kissing out there," I explain.

"Well, it'd be just like her to try to sink her nails into him now that he's going to make some real money. She was always so concerned about appearances. Hated that he was here and not some big, fancy apartment downtown," Cornelia goes on.

"He told me about that," I say as I remember Gray sharing a bit about his past with me.

"Sorry, Roxy. I hope you two kids work it out. We really thought you were a good pair," Margie adds.

"Thanks, Margie." I clear my throat because I don't want to cry in front of these women. "So, what can we help you with?"

They look at each other and Margie elbows Cornelia again.

"What's this 'why choose' thing we keep hearing about from Cam?" Cornelia asks.

Jocelyn snorts out a laugh. "This way, ladies. I know just the book for you," she says with a wink.

I press my lips together to keep from laughing.

"I mean, seriously, how many dicks can you actually fit in there?" I hear Margie's voice from behind a shelf. My body shakes with much-needed laughter.

"Well, according to this one...three," Cornelia answers.

"Oh, wait, here's an alien one," Jocelyn adds and Cornelia starts laughing.

"Holy shit! This poor woman is going to need a cigarette, a drink, and some painkillers," she says.

As much as I want to kick Gray's ass right now, I do have to admit that I love my apartment building and its residents. Tay would be glad that I'm making more friends. She's always telling me I need to put myself out there more often. I make a mental note to text her later.

"Can we make one of these the book for next month's book club?" Margie asks me as she approaches with her selection.

"I don't see why not," I say.

"You know, I have this nephew...I mean, if you want to dip your foot back into the dating pool," she offers.

I shake my head. "You know, I think I might pull myself off the market for a while. I'm sort of over men at the moment."

"Fair enough. The two of us swore off men a long time ago. I mean, other than that nice man we hired a few times, but I don't think that counts, does it? Oh and our dates from the app the other night," she says.

"Hired?" I ask, frowning in confusion.

Cornelia swats Margie's arm as she walks over to us with Jocelyn in tow. "Margie!"

"What? The girls can keep a secret," Margie says. "We found this escort right after our husbands died. I mean, ladies have needs. He offered us a two-for-one, but Cornelia said no way, so we both had a go with him. Cost a pretty penny."

Jocelyn bends over in a fit of laughter. "You...hired...a...sex worker...for both...of you," she manages in between laughing.

"Yep. And I don't regret it one bit. Best damn sex of my life." Margie leans forward. "Maybe you should too. I can give you his number. He's very professional."

"I'm sure he is," I say, my face flushing with heat.

"You two have a nice day," Margie adds as she takes her book.

"You think Heath is still working?" Cornelia asks as they leave.

I look over at Jocelyn who has now fallen to the floor in laughter. "I'm sorry...I just...oh God, that is some good stuff," she stammers around her laughter.

I roll my eyes. "I'm going to get a coffee. Can you pull yourself together long enough to man the desk?"

"Only if you get me this Heath's number," she teases.

I groan. "Thank you," I say as I glare at her but then our eyes meet and we both laugh. "I'm never going to look at them the same way, ever again."

"That makes two of us," Jocelyn agrees.

And with that, I head over to get coffee. I try not to glance up at Gray's apartment, but I do and I find him staring down at me. I turn away, pretending I didn't see him, but I feel his eyes boring into me the entire way across the street. Deep regret washes over me. Why did I have to fall for my neighbor? And when will I stop wanting him?

CHAPTER TWENTY-SIX

Grayson

I stare out the window waiting for Roxy to walk back across the street. I should be putting the finishing touches on my composition that Pierce and Wade wanted for the ending credits, but instead, I'm hoping to get just a small view of the woman I've fallen for. Shit. Do I love Roxy? No. It's too soon. It's hardly been two months since we first met.

A knock at my door pulls my attention from the street. I look through the peephole and sigh.

Opening the door, I glare at my friend. "What?"

"Wow. Good to see you too. Uh, any chance you can watch Ava? She's off school today and I just got called into the ER early," Bray says as I look down and see Ava peeking through his legs.

"Hi, Mr. Gray," Ava says shyly as she looks inside my apartment. She's been in here a few times. Mostly, she just wants to play the piano or watch television. I did teach her

Three Blind Mice on the cello a few months ago, but she bored of that after twenty minutes.

"Hi, Ava," I reply as I step to the side and put a hand out, motioning them inside. It's then I notice Bray has a small pink book bag. Ava giggles and runs through his legs and into my apartment.

"Aves! Do not run!" he yells after her. But she's already spinning in circles so her skirt puffs up.

"Look at my skirt, Mr. Gray! I'm a ballerina!" she yells.

"Did you fill her up on sugar before bringing her here?" I ask as I stare at the whirlwind that is Ava.

Bray smirks. "Nope."

"We got ice cream!" she yells as she stops spinning and falls on the ground, spreading out her limbs like a starfish and making a fake snow angel.

"Great," I say sarcastically, glaring at Bray who just hands me the bag.

"Thanks. I owe you. Carly will be home in like two hours. Later, Aves!" Bray says.

She gets up and runs over to hug him. He picks her up and twirls her around and she laughs. Then he sets her down and they do some ridiculous handshake thing that ends with bumping hips.

I roll my eyes as Bray leaves.

"Whatcha doing?" Ava asks as she looks around my apartment.

I run a hand through my hair. "Well, I was going to work on some music."

"Can I help?" she asks as she points to my cello. "I think I still remember that song you taught me."

I chuckle as I watch her walk over to examine the bow. "Unfortunately, I have to play something a little more complicated than that song. How about we go to the park? I can finish this later."

"Really?" she asks, her eyebrows shooting up as she walks back over to me.

"Sure. Why not?"

She does a fist pump. "Yes!" Looking up at me, she adds, "I love the park. Can we feed the ducks?"

At the end of the trail in the park, there's a duck pond. And all the kids love feeding the ducks.

"I suppose. Come on," I say as I grab my keys and set her bag down. Fortunately, Licorice has remained elusive or we'd never be leaving.

We walk downstairs and she runs out the front door.

"Ava! Hold up!" I call out as I shut the door. I freeze when my eyes lock with Roxy's.

"Miss Roxy!" Ava calls out as she runs over and wraps her arms around Roxy's thighs.

"Oh, uh, hey, Ava," Roxy stammers as her gaze continues to stay fixated on me.

"We're going to the park. You wanna come with us?" Ava asks with a big smile. Fuck. This kid is adorable. She has zero idea that an entire building of adults would gladly step in front of oncoming traffic for her. "Please!" she adds while giving her best puppy dog eyes.

Roxy slowly changes her focus from me to Ava. "Well, cutie pie, I have to work. But maybe another time. I'm sure you'll have plenty of fun with Mr. Gray."

Ava waves her hand at me. "Mr. Gray is just Mr. Gray, but you...you're much cooler."

"Hey!" I protest, suddenly feeling very jealous of Roxy for completely unrealistic reasons. I'm about to say more when the door opens and Al walks out. Ava spins around and runs straight into Al's open arms. He chuckles and tosses her into the air as if she weighs nothing and he's half his age. Then she wraps her arms around his neck and nuzzles her face against his cheek.

"Good afternoon, Miss Ava," Al says in his gravelly old voice.

"Do you want to come with Mr. Gray and me to feed the ducks?" she asks as she leans back and looks at him. I swear their interaction makes me want a kid and at the same time I feel bad that my future kids won't have a grandparent like Al. He's the best.

Al glances over at me and I shrug. "The more the merrier," I say.

"I suppose I could use a walk. Lead the way, young lady," he says as he sets her down. He looks over at Roxy. "You joining us?"

She shakes her head and motions to the store. "Not today, Al. I have some things to get done. But you guys have fun."

Al looks between us and I can see him trying to figure out what is going on. Great. Now, I'm about to get the Spanish Inquisition.

"Let's go find these ducks, then. See you later, Roxy," Al says as Ava grabs his hand and they begin walking down the street.

I pause next to Roxy. I want to talk to her, but I can't do that and babysit Ava.

"Have fun," she says and quickly darts around me and into her store. I stare after her, filled with regret. Damn. I fucked up.

I hurry along to catch up with Al and Ava.

"What's going on with you two?" Al asks.

"Nothing," I mumble.

"That didn't look like nothing," he quips.

"It's just a...misunderstanding," I say, trying to remain vague because I don't want to get into it.

He opens his mouth to speak again but my phone buzzes. It's Pierce. "Can you take her down to the pond? I'll be there in a minute," I promise.

He nods but pauses as he steps toward Ava. Turning back to me, he says, "Don't let a disagreement disentangle you from the best thing that ever happened to you. Whatever it is between you, it's very real. Anyone can see that you belong together. Remember that."

He gives me a knowing look and then he turns and the two of them continue down the trail. I sit next to the now-empty bench. Someone must have taken the flowers today.

"Hey," I answer before the call goes to voicemail.

"So, how's that piece coming along? I was hoping you'd be able to send it over tonight," he says. "Wade and I want to listen to it."

"Sure. I just have something to finish up here and then I'll get it over to you," I assure him. Carly better not be late.

"Great." He pauses. Fuck, is this where he's going to bring up the Roxy thing which I one hundred percent am sure Haven has told him about. "About Roxy," he starts. Yep. Damn it. "I really don't care if you were together or not. You could have just told me, man."

I run a hand through my hair. "I'm sorry, Pierce. I sort of over-spoke and then it blew up into this thing. It's my bad. I should have just been upfront with you."

"Yes. You should have been." He pauses again. "I hope this isn't overstepping, but for whatever it's worth, you two are perfect together. I sort of figured out that first night that you weren't really together, but any idiot could see you both were attracted to each other. Don't let that one get away, Grayson. She's the real deal."

OK, well, that wasn't what I thought he'd say. And damn, is it that obvious to everyone that we were so good together?

"Oh, uh, right. Thanks, Pierce," is all I manage to say.

"We'll talk later," Pierce says and he ends the call, leaving me sitting on the bench in total confusion.

"Now what?" I say to myself.

Hutch's voice comes out of a nearby tree. "Now you need to figure out how to get the girl, you big dumbass."

"Hutch?" I ask as I look around.

"I'm on this video monitor," he says. "Freaking thing hasn't caught anyone yet. It somehow got disconnected this morning."

"Fuck, you need to let this go. Just let the flower thing be a mystery," I say into a small camera I find tied to a nearby tree.

"No can do. Also, you need to win Roxy back. Pierce is right. She's the real deal and you were so happy when you were with her," his voice says.

He's not wrong. And I sort of hate myself right now.

"How?" I ask.

I can practically hear him grinning. "That's the spirit. No idea. But we'll figure it out."

CHAPTER TWENTY-SEVEN

Roxy

I flip through the mail as Isla and Jocelyn chat over a cup of tea. Isla was nearby to do some shopping and decided to stop in for a visit. I have to admit, it's nice to see her.

"So, you all ready for the official grand opening?" she asks me as she sets her tea down.

I shrug. I pushed the date back a bit. Sales have been a little slow and I really wanted to do something big, something different. I have a few authors ready to attend and sign, but it feels like it's not enough and I'm getting nervous.

"Sort of," I admit to my sister. I've been trying to be better about talking with my parents and siblings. They have shown over the past few months how supportive they are and how proud they are of me. It's taking time to recognize that I have the same potential as all of them. But I'm getting there, slowly. My recent revelations are helping me.

"It'll be great. I mean, if it's half as good as your soft opening night, then it'll be amazing," she says.

I feel my cheeks heat a little under her praise. Fuck, I really am lucky to have such awesome siblings.

"So, what's up with Gray? I saw him talking to you the other day," Jocelyn prods.

"I thought you said you two broke up," Isla says as she leans back in her chair.

Sighing, I run my finger around the rim of my mug. "We did."

I have told my family that Gray and I just didn't work out, but I haven't said why. Jocelyn, on the other hand, knows everything. I've even called Tay to vent a few times. Not that it has made me feel any better.

I hear our mailman, Bernie Summers, humming as he drops some envelopes into the store's mail slot. Must be a light mail day. Normally, I have bigger packages, and he comes in and drops them at the desk.

I walk from my apartment into the store and grab the mail from the little basket I secured by the slot to catch things. As I glance at the envelopes on my way back to my dining area, I see a letter addressed to Kasen Saddler. Frowning, I look at the return address. It's blank.

Huh.

"What's that look for?" Jocelyn asks as I sit down and rifle through the rest of my mail.

"Nothing, just got a letter addressed to Kasen. I suppose I can slide it under his door. I have no idea when he'll be back," I explain as I look down again at his name on the envelope.

"Has anyone heard from him?" Jocelyn asks.

"What's going on?" Isla says as she looks from Jocelyn to me. I launch into the weird missing-neighbor situation or non-communicative-neighbor situation, and by the time I finish, I realize how badly I want to tell Gray that I got this letter.

"Why don't you give it to Brayden or Hutch?" Jocelyn suggests.

"I guess I could. It's so weird, right?" I state as I flip the letter over and then place it on the table.

Shrugging, she turns to Isla and asks her about her graduate program. The two fall quickly into a conversation about grad schools and my mind drifts to Grayson. When Richard cheated on me, I was heartbroken. I thought I'd never find a man as good as him. I thought I was undeserving of love.

But then Grayson came into my life. The last two months he burrowed his way into my heart. He was kind and respectful...other than our meet-cute. He's far from perfect, but so am I. The closeness I felt with him was unlike anything I'd felt before. When he listened to me, he heard me, truly heard me. The way he made love to me, the way he kissed me, it was all-consuming. I never would have thought he'd kiss his ex. How did I miss that? Was I so wrapped up in opening my store that I couldn't see past it to what was happening in my love life? Maybe.

God, this sucks! Everything was so perfect for like two seconds. I had a great place to live. I had finally opened my dream store. I had a great employee, good friends, and wonderful neighbors, and I was finally starting to feel seen by my family. Everything was so much better, for a second. And Grayson was like the cherry on top.

My heart aches again as my mind recalls Gray kissing Lydia.

The memory is cut short when the bell on my store's door dings. I peek around the open door between my apartment and my shop. Brayden. I frown because Brayden, other than quickly stopping by the soft opening, is not a romance reader and hasn't been shopping in here.

"I'll be right back," I say to Jocelyn and Isla. Jocelyn leans forward in her chair, seeing Brayden, she looks curiously between us and then continues talking with my sister.

I close the door a little as I walk up to him.

"Hey, Brayden. What can I help you with?" I ask, looking around us as if the reasoning for his visit will become obvious.

He runs his hand through his hair, reminding me a bit of Grayson. He's slightly shorter than Grayson, maybe closer to six feet, and has the build of a runner who might do a little weight training on the side. I can't help wondering if there could be something more between him and Carly. They'd be so perfect together.

"I think you should see something," he says as he pulls his phone out of his pocket. I watch him unlock it as he continues to speak. "I was friends with Gray when Lydia broke his heart. I was seeing this woman off and on and we all used to go out together on occasion. Lydia tolerated me because I was a doctor and I suppose for her, that's socially acceptable. After what happened the other day, I texted her to tell her exactly what I thought of her behavior."

He hands me the phone and I look down at a text conversation.

"Go on, read it," he encourages.

Brayden: What the fuck, Lydia? Why would you kiss Gray? That's really fucked up.

I have to stop myself from laughing when I see what he has named Lydia on his phone.

Golddigger Dragon Lady: I don't know what you are talking about.

Brayden: Gray told me everything.

Golddigger Dragon Lady: Well, did he tell you that he kissed me back? We aren't over yet. Even he knows this. He just needed to get rid of that low-life smut seller. So I did it for him. He'll come around eventually.

Brayden: So you kissed him on purpose, knowing that Roxy would see it?

Golddigger Dragon Lady: Obviously. I could have heard her coming a mile away. Her shoes were absolutely vulgar. Anyhow, now that Gray has figured out how wrong she was for him, we can get back together. You know we were good together, Bray. We were happy. I just...needed some time. We were young.

Brayden: Lydia, that was only a year ago.

Golddigger Dragon Lady: So what? I thought you'd be on my side. I thought we were friends.

Brayden: Yes, I thought we *were* friends too until you broke my best friend's heart over how much money he was making. Go fuck yourself.

I look up at Brayden. "I didn't know you still spoke to her," I say as I try to wrap my head around what I just read while handing him his phone back.

"We don't. I just didn't delete her number from my phone," he explains. "And I'm glad I didn't because now you know the truth."

Blowing out a long breath, I cross my arms. "OK, fine, so he didn't kiss her, but he still is blaming me for Pierce finding out we were fake dating. I'm not good with that either."

He cocks his head to one side as he considers what I've said. "I get that. He was upset and he should have thought his words through before speaking to you. You should know by now that Gray can be a little hot-tempered at times."

"A little?" I say with a pointed look.

He chuckles. "Fine, a lot. But it's only because he's a passionate person. He fights with words and sometimes he lets his emotions get the better of him. It's probably his only fault. If it's any consolation, I think he feels terrible."

I look around us. "Well, I don't see him here apologizing."

"You could go talk to him," he says.

Groaning, I look down at my feet. I hate that he's not wrong, but I also am stubborn, maybe that's *my* biggest fault. "I could, but I'm not going to. He came raging in here all mad when I was already mad at him, and he knew it."

"I think you should talk to him. I promise you, Roxy, he's worth it. You will never find a more loyal, kind, smart, funny, and passionate man. I've watched him go above and beyond for his friends. He's a good man and I've seen you two together. You had something real. Don't toss it away over his crazy ex and one misunderstanding," Brayden says as he starts to turn to leave.

I contemplate his words for a second but then remember Kasen's letter.

"Brayden?"

He turns back to me, and I hold up a finger as I walk to the door in the back. I open it and Isla and Jocelyn scurry to their seats. "Seriously? Eavesdropping?"

Jocelyn shrugs and Isla looks sheepish. I roll my eyes and grab the mail.

Walking back to him, I shove it in his hand. "This is for Kasen. No idea how it got mixed in with mine."

Frowning, Brayden looks at it, turning it over just like I did. "Weird. Uh, thanks. I'll slide it under his door."

"Oh, I could have done that," I say, not sure what I expected.

"I can do it," he assures me as he waves the letter. He walks out of my store, and I stand there watching him go, wondering where I went wrong. Am I to blame for how things went down with Gray? No. Maybe? I did immediately jump to conclusions. And I do feel bad about that now. He was trying to tell me the truth and I wouldn't listen. Fuck. Is it too late?

CHAPTER TWENTY-EIGHT

Grayson

Hutch, Bray, and I sit at the bar waiting for Al to serve us our Thursday drinks.

"So, how are we getting you two back together?" Hutch asks as he grabs his drink from Al.

All eyes turn on me and a hush falls over everyone including Margie, Cornelia, Jessa, Troy, Cam, Carly, Drew, and even Ava. According to Cam, Roxy had to go pick up a last-minute shipment, so she won't be here for a while. I've been trying to figure out a way to talk to her. To apologize for being an ass, to plead with her to give us a second chance. But I haven't figured out a way to do that yet.

The door to the stairwell swings open and Jocelyn walks out, looking at all of us as we turn to see her.

"Uh, hi, I…" She trails off and looks around.

"Hey, come on over," Al says warmly with a wave of his hand.

She walks over to us and stands at the end of the bar. She looks straight at me, and again, everyone is silent.

"How are you going to fix this?" she asks as her eyes search mine.

"Yeah, Gray, how *are* you fixing this?" Hutch mimics as he leans over Bray to look at me.

I run my hand through my hair. "You're freaking him out. Give him a minute. The boy needs to think," Cornelia says as she gets up and walks over to me, patting my shoulder. She leans closer and whispers in my ear, "You do have a plan, don't you?"

I close my eyes and sigh. How am I the last one to have known? Why did it take us fighting for me to realize Roxy is the best thing in my life? She likes me for me. It's not about my family or their money or even my career. She just liked me for who I am. And I need that in my life.

"We can help," Al offers. There's a rash of nods and "yeses" from my neighbors.

"Bro, you need a giant-ass grand gesture," Drew quips from where he sits behind me. "I mean like a motherfucking, sorry, Aves, mother-effing huge book boyfriend grand gesture."

"That's OK, Mr. Drew," Ava says from where she is coloring at the table next to him. "What's a grand gesture?"

"It's like...crud, I can't think of a cartoon grand gesture," Carly muses as she taps her cheek, deep in thought.

"Oh, uh, remember how the Beast gave Belle that library? That's like a grand gesture," Drew says.

"Dude, that's not a grand gesture. It was that ball thing when they danced," Hutch says.

"No, it was when he fought off that jerk guy," Cam interjects.

"Mommy, I still don't get it," Ava whispers.

Carly laughs. "It's OK. I'm fairly certain I'm confused now too."

"Oh, Mr. Gray?" Ava says and I turn to look at her. "Miss Roxy likes books. Why don't you get her a book?" Her face lights up. "Or take her to see that new movie. Mommy, what's that new movie you and Mr. Drew were talking about? Mr. Drew said it's an apatation."

"Adaptation," everyone corrects simultaneously.

"Yeah, that," Ava says. "What is that?"

"It's when a book is made into a movie," Carly says as she and Bray exchange smiles. God, those two need to hook up and get it over with.

"Movies are books?" Ava asks, her eyes wide.

"Some movies are," Bray answers.

"Cool," Ava replies with a grin.

My mind starts to spin. A movie. Shit, Pierce's other project is working on a film adaptation of this super famous romance book. He had mentioned last week that the film tour was wrapping up here next week. We had been discussing when our film's press tour would start and he had said it was perfect timing with the other one finishing up now. Roxy's grand opening is supposed to be next week, although word on the street is she was wanting to push it back because she was worried what she had planned wouldn't be enough. Which it is, but maybe, just maybe, I can help make it better.

"I have an idea," I say slowly as I pull my phone out of my pocket.

"I love ideas," Al says excitedly.

I press call on my phone. "Pierce?" I say when he picks up. "I need a favor."

———

I've spent all week making arrangements. At first, I wanted to tell Roxy and take all the credit for what I'm doing, but I changed my mind almost as fast as the idea had come to me. I don't want to make this about me. This is her day. So in the end, I had Pierce and Haven agree to take credit for the idea. Haven worked with Roxy and set up a visit for the grand opening from not only the bestselling author of the recent film adaptation but also two of the film's actors. Jocelyn says Roxy is ecstatic and that the event is looking to be absolutely beyond anything Roxy has imagined.

That made me smile.

It's the morning of the grand opening. It's also the day that I've turned in my last score edits for the film. When I wasn't working with Pierce to get actors to Roxy's shop, I was working with the local orchestra to record the final musical score for the film. Wade just sent me the files and it's beyond my wildest dreams. For the first time in my life, I'm proud of my work. I did that.

My phone rings and it's Pierce.

"Hey, just got the final files," I answer.

"You want to see them in action?" Pierce asks.

"You mean, you added them already?" I ask in confusion. I knew Pierce was working with his editor on the film, but I had no idea they had a rough cut ready.

"Yep," he replies.

"Hell, yeah, I do," I laugh, still feeling like this is all a dream.

The call switches to a video chat and I accept. I'm greeted by a large monitor.

"Here you are. I'd invite you over, but I'm too stoked to wait any longer," he explains as he hits play and my music fills the silence on the call like a misty fog rolling across a valley. I'm encased and enraptured by it; I watch the opening scene unfold as crescendos build drama. My heart thunders in my chest, only slowing as the music ends.

"And here." Pierce fast-forwards to the next scene with music. He does this again and again until we reach the ending credits.

It's quiet as he presses pause following the last note of a moving piece of music that I created after the first night Roxy and I slept together. I was so inspired that I changed my score, and when I shared it with Wade and Pierce, they immediately green-lighted it for recording.

Pierce turns the camera to his face. "You nailed it. Everyone is going to want to use you. You have no idea what is coming your way. My advice...enjoy these next few weeks because your life is about to change in a major way. And you deserve it. I knew you would be the perfect fit for this production. But you exceeded even my wildest expectations. Congrats!"

I shake my head in disbelief. "Thanks. I...don't even know what to say," I admit. "Just, thanks for taking a chance on me, for believing in me. I don't know how to repay you for that."

"You did that. Your insistence and bugging me got you in my door and the rest is just, well, it's your talent. This is your moment to shine." He pauses and smiles at me. "I believe you have a big day today. Haven and I will be there at one sharp."

"I'll see you both there. Wish me luck," I say.

"You don't need it. She may be mad at you, but she loves you. It's clear to anyone who has seen you together. You'll see," he promises and I hope what he says is true. Love...shit, yeah, I love her too. God, I hope he's right.

Licorice meows and I look down at her. "Hey, you ready to go see your mom?" I may have gotten her a cute cat outfit. It's taken a few days to acclimate her to it, but she'll at least walk around with it on now.

I get myself dressed in a suit because Roxy commented on my suit one night and that stuck with me. So many of her passing comments stick with me. She has no idea how much I've come to need her, to crave her in my life. I've been an empty shell for days. How did she weasel her way into my heart so quickly? I thought for sure after Lydia broke up with me that I'd never love another woman. But Roxy changed me, and for the better.

I get Licorice dressed next and in her harness, and then I look in the mirror.

"Ready?" I ask her. She meows back and I laugh, already feeling lighter just knowing I'll be in the presence of the woman who has stolen my fucking heart.

"Let's do this," I say more to myself than the cat. I grab the flowers sitting on the side table by my front door and we walk downstairs. Through the glass of the front door, I can see that the sidewalk is packed with people, a line stretches down the street. Holy shit! I had no idea it would be this crazy. I pull out my phone and call Troy.

"Hey, man, what's up?" he answers on the first ring.

"I need a favor. I need you to let me in the side entrance to the bookstore," I say.

"Er, I don't think I can. Sorry. Maybe try the front door?" he suggests.

"Troy, look out the window," I growl.

He's quiet for a beat. "Fuck. That's a lot of people. Sorry. Maybe you can ask to skip the line, I see a limo pulling up, pretend you're with them."

A limo. "That's actually not a bad idea," I state as I walk out the front door and see Pierce and Haven following two actors, another woman who I assume is the author and their entourage.

"Hey," Haven says when she sees me.

I look at the line and back at Haven. "Any chance I can come inside with you all?"

Haven grins and winks at me. "Of course, just follow behind us."

I nod and get in line behind them as security ushers us inside. Damn, she even hired a security guy for the front door.

Pierce leans into me as we approach the door. "I paid for some security. Glad I did," he says with a laugh as the people in line start screaming when the two actors approach them. The actors take it in stride, walking down the roped-off line and taking selfies with fans. They come back after a few moments, promising more when the fans get inside. I follow them all into the store. If the soft launch was awesome, this is ten times better. An area in back has six tables with signing authors. The two actors have a backdrop area just to the left of the desk. There's a table with giveaway bags. Outside, two food and ice cream trucks have pulled up to serve customers. A coffee bar is set up inside and she's added a special editions section for opening day.

"Wow!" I say as I continue to look around until my eyes lock on two familiar blue ones. Roxbury Benedict looks like a wet dream. She's in a red dress. Her gorgeous hair hangs down in loose curls. And those heels should be illegal. Her gaze meets mine and we just stare at each other for a long beat. The whole world disappears for long seconds. And I know without a doubt that I will do anything to win her back. If this doesn't work, I'll show up here every day from now until eternity.

CHAPTER TWENTY-NINE

Roxy

I blink a few times because, with all of the excitement of the day, I swear I might be hallucinating right now. But no, he doesn't disappear. Gray is standing in front of me, with Licorice on a leash and in a dress, a freaking cat dress. He's holding a bouquet of roses, and damn it, he looks like a real-life book boyfriend in his three-piece suit.

He steps toward me as the actors come up to meet me. I try my best to give them my full attention and thank Pierce and Haven. Jocelyn sidles up beside me along with her friend Clare who I hired part-time to help this week, and longer if things pick up at the store.

I keep watching Gray every few seconds out of the corner of my eye. He waits patiently as I make sure everyone is situated.

"Shall we let people in?" Jocelyn asks, motioning to the front door.

"One last thing," he says as he steps up beside her, looking at me with such intensity I feel my face heat. I suddenly wish we were alone so he could strip me right out of this dress and I could slowly unbutton that crisp white shirt, vest, and jacket. I know what lies beneath it, and damn have I missed that. Hell, I've missed everything about him if I'm being honest with myself. But this isn't the time or the place for us to talk...or do anything else.

Clearing my throat, I compose myself as I glance around us. "Grayson, we really need to get..." I trail off as he hands me the flowers he's been holding.

"Licorice and I wanted to congratulate you," he states. I smile as I look from him to Licorice, and then I lean down to pet her. Licorice rubs against my hand as I stand back up and look into his eyes once again.

"Thank you, Gray," I whisper as I accept them, allowing myself to breathe in the scent of the flowers before Jocelyn is there to take them away.

"I'll get a vase," she says quietly as she steps toward the back of the store.

"I need to..." I trail off as I look around us again. His hand comes up and gently strokes my cheek.

"I know. I'll let you get to it, Roxbury. I just wanted you to know how proud of you I am." He pauses and follows my gaze around the store. Roxbury. He said my full name and something about that makes me fall even harder for him. Fighting my feelings is getting more difficult by the second. "*You* did all of this. Don't ever forget that." He motions with his hand.

I blush. "Thank you."

"Enjoy it. We'll see you later," he says as he steps back, and suddenly I don't want him to leave. I want him right here with me. My heart aches with need for him.

I reach out and grab his arm. "Wait. Uh, don't leave. Have a seat or drop Licorice off at home and come back down.

There's more to say. I...it's just a bad time at the moment," I stammer.

He nods. "OK," he replies as he steps to the side. We meet gazes one last time before I turn to the room.

"Everyone ready?" I ask. I get a bunch of "yeses." "Great. Thank you all for being here from the bottom of my heart. I hope you enjoy yourselves, and if there's anything you need, just ask Jocelyn, Clare, or me."

There's a round of applause and then I give the security guy a nod and the doors open. I watch as Gray sneaks out while one by one, my patrons come into the store.

Haven walks up to me and links our arms. "Congrats. And when you have time, after today, please go talk to him. He's done so much for today that you don't even know about. That man loves you, Roxy. Mark my words, he's one of the great ones. Do *not* let him get away."

She squeezes my arm and walks back over to Pierce, leaving me with my mouth agape until a reader I recognize comes over to talk with me. Holy shit! Did Gray have something to do with the actors in my store? My mind races a mile a minute, but I don't have time to contemplate it more as I greet my patrons.

———

The last customer walks out of the store and Jocelyn locks the door. We are the only two people here and it's nearly eight. Seven long hours, but it was so worth it.

"We can clean up in the morning before we open. Clare said she could come by," Jocelyn says as she powers down our tablet. I glance at my phone for the time in hours and see missed texts from some family and friends, including Tay, who I feel I've barely spoken to lately. I make a silent promise to do better with balancing my work and personal life. I set the phone back down.

"Great," I say as I take off my heels and stretch my toes. "How in the hell do women wear these things all day every day?"

"They have a pain kink?" she replies with a laugh.

I giggle and shake my head at her.

I slip on some flats that are way more comfortable as I flit around the store and put things away. My mind cycles through the events of the day. It was so amazing. I can't believe I had such a huge turnout. We had a local news crew cover it and two local papers had reporters stop by. I can't believe how many people came today. It gives me hope that this silly, old dream of mine might just work out after all.

"Roxy?" Jocelyn's voice breaks me away from my thoughts.

"Yes?"

"I think Gray is waiting for you," she says as she points out the window. I walk over and peer out in the direction of the park. He's sitting on the bench with the flowers, and I'm shocked to find the flowers still there next to him.

"I'll see you tomorrow," she says as she walks out of the store, leaving me looking down the street at Gray. I take a few deep breaths to calm myself, lock up the store, and walk down the street. The cool evening air has me hugging myself as I walk up to the edge of the park and take a seat next to the flowers.

"You left," I say to him as I glance over to find him watching me.

"You were busy. I didn't want to bother you," he replies.

We sit in silence for a long minute. Eventually, I look down at the note on the flowers. It's definitely the ones that are always here, but the note today is a little different.

They are red roses and peonies. And the note reads:

Today's flowers represent love. Love isn't easy. It is filled with difficult moments. But it endures nonetheless. It's also fragile. Take care of it. Let the other person into your heart. You may regret many things in life, but you won't regret that.

~The Guardian of Hearts Lane Park

I look up at him. "Did you leave these here?" I ask.

He shakes his head. "No," he says quietly.

I pick up the flowers and set them aside, scooting over to sit next to him. I can smell his cologne and feel the heat of his body. Something about that is immensely comforting.

"Thank you for bringing Licorice today, and for the flowers...and everything else," I say. He searches my eyes. "I'm sorry, Gray. I shouldn't have jumped to conclusions. I...I'm sorry."

His hand comes up to cup my cheek. "I'm sorry too. I was angry and I should have waited to speak to you. It wasn't fair."

I laugh as I feel my eyes well with tears. "We're a mess."

He smiles at me and my heart warms. "We're definitely a mess."

We sit there grinning at each other. Not speaking, not moving, just connecting in some strangely perfect way.

"For the love of God, will you two just kiss and finish making up already!" Hutch's disembodied voice comes out of a nearby tree.

I jump back a bit and look around us. "Hutch?" I say as I frown in confusion.

"Seriously," Gray mutters as he turns to the tree beside us and stands. I watch him rip a small camera off a branch. "No more spying."

"Oh, come on. Yeah, things were just getting good," I hear Cam's voice.

"I vote for you to kiss her," Al says.

"How many of you are watching this?" he asks.

"All of us. It took you two long enough," Margie says.

I'm now shaking with laughter, doubled over on the bench, trying to catch my breath. "I...can't. Why are you all watching us?" I finally manage as Gray walks over to me.

"We wanted to make sure the grand gesture worked," Al explains.

"What grand gesture? The flowers and cat?" I ask in confusion.

"OK, everyone, thanks for the help. We're signing off now," Gray says, and he flips a small switch on the side of the device, but not before I hear Cornelia say, "We've got night-vision binoculars at our place."

Gray and I burst out laughing.

"Dear God," I say once my tears subside. I wipe under my eyes.

"Come on, let's go have a drink at my place, where people won't be using night-vision binoculars to watch us," Gray offers as he stands and holds out his hand to me.

I accept it and he pulls me up against him. "Gray," I start.

"Yes, wifey," he says.

Grinning, I lean back a little so we can look at each other. "I don't think I was ever faking romance with you. I think I started falling for you when I first saw you watching me in your window."

He leans down and presses his forehead to mine. "I wasn't faking either. You drive me crazy, but...I guess that's why I love you."

I feel my eyes tear up again but this time it's with tears of joy. "You love me?" I whisper.

"Yes," he replies.

"I love you too," I admit.

He leans down and kisses me and in the distance I hear cheering, we both laugh through the kiss, and when we pull back, I see the love in his eyes. I've never seen that from a man before, not like how he's looking at me. This is real; it was real the entire time.

He takes my hand, and we begin to walk back to one-eleven Hearts Lane.

"By the way," I say, "you really didn't need to organize movie stars to attend my grand opening. That was a bit over the top for a grand gesture."

"You knew?" he asks.

"I figured it out," I admit.

He pulls me against him, stopping us in the middle of the sidewalk. "I guess I'll need to come up with a bigger, grander gesture, then," he muses.

"Nah"—I pause—"or maybe you could just write me a song or something and have it played in a movie."

He chuckles and kisses my nose. "I'll work on that."

"Good, because now that you made a grand gesture, you still have to keep this love alive. I have some books you could read, I mean, if you need some inspiration," I say with a wink.

"Oh, you have some books, huh?"

"Yeah, something like that," I reply as I lean up and kiss him. This time when our neighbors hoot and holler, we don't stop, because we don't hear them, the world is just Gray and me.

EPILOGUE

Roxy

Four weeks later…

"Get back in here," Gray says as he grabs me and pulls me down on the bed with him. I squeal.

"Hey, we need to get dressed for happy hour," I protest. Clare and Jocelyn are manning the store this afternoon, so I snuck up here to visit with Gray.

I feel the length of his erection against my thigh, and I reach between us and stroke him. He groans. "You're killing me, wifey. I thought you said we needed to get dressed."

"We do, in a minute," I tease, feeling his hard length against my fingertips.

"Damn, a minute. Way to kill a man's ego," he says, his breath hot against my ear.

I push him a little and he rolls over, allowing me to climb on top of him and impale myself. We both let out a moan as I sink down onto his erection. I'm not sure I will ever get tired of this.

"Fuck, you feel good," he curses.

We both stop talking as he grips my hips, guiding me up and down his length. It definitely takes more than a minute.

When we finish, I fall against him, resting my head on his chest, while feeling him still deep inside me. I feel safe and loved and part of me doesn't want to go to happy hour, but eventually, I roll off him.

Licorice jumps up and meows at us.

"I think someone wants to come with us," Gray says. I giggle as Licorice rubs her head against my hand. She's become quite fond of going for walks and also spending time at happy hour. She also likes sleeping on the chair by the window in my shop. She's essentially one-eleven Hearts Lane's mascot.

I get up and walk into the bathroom, turning on the shower. We make quick work of washing each other before throwing on our clothes.

"I'll put her harness on," Gray says as we finish dressing. He gets Licorice ready, and we head upstairs. Everyone is already sipping drinks and chatting as we take two seats at the bar.

"Awww! Licorice!" Ava cries out as she runs over to play with our cat. Al tosses her one of Licorice's cat toys he's hoarded under his bar.

"You're spoiling her," I tease as I take my drink from Al.

"Hardly, that cat's our last line of defense against mice and bugs. She deserves more cat treats," Al says.

"Hey, I just got the exterminator to come last week. He says our building is great compared to at least five others on the street," Troy protests.

"I'm joking, Troy. We all know you care for this building like it's your baby, and that's why I hired you," Al says, his voice softening.

"It's a big, pain-in-my-ass baby," Troy grumbles under his breath.

Everyone laughs.

"How's that camera thing going?" Brayden asks Hutch.

"It's not. I lost like two cameras to trash pandas, and another one got taken by some kids on scooters," Hutch huffs.

"So, you giving up?" Drew asks.

"Hell no. I will get to the bottom of it," Hutch promises.

"Get to the bottom of what?" a deep voice calls out from the stairwell door.

The entire rooftop goes completely silent as everyone's heads swivel toward the doorway.

It only takes me five seconds to realize who the man standing there is…it's Kasen. I recognize him from photos.

"Holy shitballs! You *are* alive!" Drew yells.

Cam and Carly run over and hug him, followed by Jessa, Margie, and Cornelia. Soon everyone is standing around Kasen as if he's a long-lost soldier who has just returned from war.

Kasen greets everyone and then his eyes lock with mine. "I don't believe we've met," he says as he holds out a hand.

I blush and shake his hand. "I'm Roxy. I own the bookstore downstairs and live in the studio."

"Oh, right, Al said he was leasing out the commercial space. Nice to meet you," he replies as he looks at Gray's arm that is wrapped around my shoulders.

"Nice to meet you too," I reply.

"Looks like I have some catching up to do," he says.

Cam waves her hand in the air. "Hutch is trying to solve the flower bench mystery. Al closed up the antique shop and leased it to Roxy. Roxy and Gray fake dated but now are really dating. The entire building is part of a romance book club now. Oh, and Cam may be on the verge of finally owning her own bakery."

"And I lost a tooth!" Ava squeals as she runs over and smiles up at Kasen so he can see her missing tooth.

Kasen grins at her and picks her up. She looks ridiculously small in his arms. "Wow, did the tooth fairy come?"

She nods. "I got five dollars because it was my first tooth."

"Darn! That's a lot," he says as he looks back at all of us. "So, I didn't miss much, then?"

Everyone bursts out laughing.

"Come on, I'll make you a drink and you can tell us all about where you've been," Al says.

And just like that, everyone meanders over to the bar, surrounding Kasen and asking him a million questions. But Gray and I remain where we are.

"Will our story always start with the fake-dating thing?" I whisper.

"Should we start with me yelling at you about the noise?" he asks with a raised eyebrow.

I press my lips together to keep from smiling. "No," I manage after a second.

"Well, then I guess it will, but I promise you one thing," he says.

"What's that?" I ask as I wrap my arms around his neck.

"There's nothing fake between us anymore," he adds as he leans down and kisses me.

"Ewww! Kissing!" Ava yells as everyone laughs again.

"That doesn't look fake to me," Kasen says.

"No, Kase, *that* is very much real," Al states. And then there are some more comments from other neighbors, but I don't pay attention because I'm too busy kissing my dream guy, my very own real grumpy-sunshine, enemies-to-lovers, fake-relationship, one-bed-trope, neighbor-romance book boyfriend.

. . .

I hope you enjoyed this story. If you want more romantic comedies, you can start with my Perfectly Imperfect Love Series. In Book 1, a photographer has to move in with a base-ball player. And don't forget to grab your free copy of the Meet-Cute Mishap by joining my newsletter, plus receive freebies, giveaways, and so much more!

ABOUT THE AUTHOR

USA Today & International bestselling romance author, S.E. Rose lives near Washington D.C. with her family. When she's not wrangling her cats or keeping up with her kids, she's plotting her next story.

She loves all things wine, coffee, and cats. In her non-existent free time, she enjoys traveling, going to concerts, binging on her favorite shows, and reading, especially if it's a good mystery or comedy.

Learn more about upcoming books from S.E. Rose at www.seroseauthor.com.

ALSO BY S.E. ROSE

Deceitful Destiny Series
Island (Book 1)
Secrets (Book 2)
Bravura (Book 3)
Determination (Book 4)
Home (Book 5)

The Poisoned Pawn World
A Fierce Princess
A Valiant Prince
A Wise Prince
A True King
The Overnight Naughty List

The Kingmakers of Kensington
A Man of Power
A Man of Wealth
A Man of Prestige

Perfectly Imperfect Love Series

Undeniably Perfect
Hopelessly Perfect
Romantically Perfect
Awkwardly Perfect
Reluctantly Perfect

Brides of Banneker
Scoring the One
Landing the One
Fixing the One

Once Upon a Billionaire Rom-Com Series
The Billionaire and the Librarian
The Billionaire and the Maid
The Billionaire and the Runaway

Romances in the Building Series
Faking Romance (Book 1)

Fanning the Flames Series (Co-authored with Sierra Hill)
Burned (Book 1)
Ignited (Book 2)
Scorched (Book 3)

Clearview Falls University Series (Co-authored with Sierra Hill)
Falling for the Fake Boyfriend (Book 1)
Falling for the Roommate (Book 2)
Falling for the Football Player (Book 3)

Novels
Chronicles of a Hot Mess
Chronicles of a Rockin' Mess

The Decoy
Second Start (A Holiday Springs Resort Novel)
The Road Trip Romance

Novellas & Short Stories
Neighbor in Apartment No. 5
The Tinsel Tango
The Fighter
A Polar Pursuit (Vagabond Series)
A Forward Holiday
Love in an Elevator
When It Rains, It Pours
Misery Loves Company

Want to learn more? Visit www.seroseauthor.com.